RANI REPORTS
ON THE MISSING MILLIONS

RANI REPORTS
ON THE MISSING MILLIONS

GABRIELLE & SATISH
SHEWHORAK

ROCK THE BOAT

A Rock the Boat Book

First published by Rock the Boat,
an imprint of Oneworld Publications, 2023

ISBN 978-0-86154-503-2 (paperback)
ISBN 978-0-86154-504-9 (ebook)

Typeset by Tetragon, London
Printed and bound in Great Britain by Clays Ltd, Elcograf S.p.A.

This book is a work of fiction. Names, characters, businesses, organisations, places and
events are either the product of the author's imagination or are used fictitiously. Any
resemblance to actual persons, living or dead, events, or locales is entirely coincidental.

Oneworld Publications
10 Bloomsbury Street
London WC1B 3SR
England

For Ashoka and her grandparents,
and for grandparents and
grandchildren everywhere.

CHAPTER ONE

BOOM! Nani Arrives!

I'm Rani, Rani Ramgoolam, and I love writing stories. Not made-up stories about made-up things, but real-life stories about real people and the exciting things that happen all around us. I think that finding a good story is a bit like unearthing ancient pottery, cleaning it up and piecing all the bits together. Then research as many facts about it as possible before presenting it for everyone to enjoy in a museum like the one Mum curates. She calls me a story archaeologist but she knows that I really want to be an investigative journalist.

The local newspaper, the *Camberford Herald*, had recently announced a Junior Journalist competition with a prize of a £100 book voucher and the winning entry printed in the paper itself. I'd been looking for a brilliant story to report but my notebook was still blank. The closing date was in nine days but the story would have to wait. It was Saturday, the first day of the Easter holidays, and one of my favourite people in the whole wide world was on her way!

BLOW YOUR NOSE! PULL UP YOUR SOCKS!

"Shush, Cookie! And get out of there!" I flapped my hands in an attempt to stop my African grey parrot from pecking every piece of fruit in the fruit bowl. Just then the door flew open with a bang.

KAKAKAKAKAKAKAAA! screeched Cookie as Nani exploded into the kitchen. The parrot launched into the air in a flurry of grey feathers, mango juice dripping from his beak.

"Nani!" I yelled, running over to her as she breezed into the room, sari swirling.

"Mo Coco!" Nani grabbed my shoulders and kissed me on both cheeks, gold earrings swinging as she ducked to avoid Cookie who was now flapping around the kitchen wailing like a police siren.

WAOW-WAOW-WAOW-WAOW-WAOW!

"Quiet, Cookie!" I called as I hugged Nani. "You'll give Nani a headache!"

QUIET, COOKIE! STOP THAT, COOKIE! SHUSH, COOKIE! he screeched in response, swooping over Nani's head to land on the curtain rail above the door.

MURDER! MURDER! CALL THE COPS!

"Ki manyer? How are you?" said Dad, putting a lid on the spaghetti sauce he was making, then coming over to greet Nani with a kiss on each cheek. He stopped and stared as Mum staggered into the kitchen after her, dragging two ginormous suitcases. "I thought you were just staying until the summer holidays!" He laughed. "I didn't realise you were moving in."

"Moving in?" repeated Nani as Mum gave Dad a Look before he said anything else cheeky. "This is just essentials." She flung open one of the cases to reveal tubs of pickles, chicken curry, vanilla teabags, preserved vegetables and a stack of soft roti. I tried not to laugh as Mum's face went a funny colour.

"Ayo, Mother! I *told* you not to bring food! You could have got into so much trouble at the airport. I asked Anishka to check your case before you left!"

AYO! AYO! AYO! screeched Cookie, bobbing up and down on the curtain rail.

"Oh, Anu, I packed *two* cases!" Nani grinned.

"Your sister checked the wrong one. Besides, why would I get into trouble for feeding my family? You are all far too thin!" Her gold bangles jangled as she patted her round tummy with pride.

Mum threw up her hands, rolled her eyes and shook her head all at the same time.

"Rani, stop Cookie screeching before my head explodes, then help your dad take Nani's things upstairs."

"Here, Cookie!" I called, patting my shoulder until he flew down to bury his head in my hair and nibble my hair clip. "Mum, can Nani sleep in my room with me? Please-please-please?"

"Absolutely not, you two will be chatting and giggling away the whole night. Nani will be in the guest room so we can *all* get some sleep!"

"Mersi, Coco!" Nani said as I took some of her bags. Nani always calls me Coco, which means something like "dear one" in Creole. That's the main language they speak in Mauritius – the tiny tropical island in the Indian Ocean where she lives and where Mum and Dad were born.

"Get off, lazy bones!" I laughed as Cookie bounced between the cases as we pulled them upstairs. Cookie cackled with glee and jumped on to Dad's hand.

"Ow!" he yelped, letting go of the heaviest case.

OW! OW! CALL THE COPS! Cookie screeched, surfing the case as it slid all the way back down the stairs. As it hit the floor it popped open, and jars of lotions and potions, books, clothes and jewellery erupted across the hall.

"Five detective novels!" said Dad as Cookie hid under one of Nani's bras, watching us repack everything. "Two pirate adventures, a stack of puzzle books and –" he lifted a nightdress to reveal a pile of books with couples staring lovingly at each other – "a LOT of romance! No wonder it was so heavy!"

"It's a portable library!" I giggled as I stacked the books on the shelf in the hall. Sadly they were all in French so I couldn't borrow any of the exciting-looking detective novels.

By the time we finished putting Nani's things into the room next to mine, scrumptious smells were drifting up the stairs. I popped Cookie into the living room. Cooking fumes can make birds very ill so he knew he had to stay out of the way whenever we made food.

POOR COOKIE. GO TO PRISON. POOR COOKIE, he grumbled. He hopped on to the perch in his huge cage and tucked his head under his wing.

"Don't be so dramatic," I said as he peeked out at me. "I haven't even shut the door!"

Back in the kitchen, Nani had pushed Dad's pan of spaghetti sauce aside to heat up some curry and roti bread while Mum brewed a pot of vanilla tea. Whenever I taste vanilla I think of Mauritius – its mountains, palm trees, sparkling blue sea, the breeze rippling through the sugar-cane fields. But the best thing about Mauritius was now right here – Nani!

"Manzer, manzer! Eat, eat!" said Nani as she filled my plate. "This chicken flew six thousand miles to feed you. Don't disappoint it."

I tore off a piece of roti and used it as a spoon to scoop up a mouthful of spicy curry.

As we ate, Nani told us what all of my cousins, aunties and uncles were doing now – who had got married recently, who had fallen out with each other. It took a *long* time as Mum has six brothers and sisters and they all have children. Cookie flew in halfway through the meal and sat on the back of Nani's chair, head tilted to one side as though listening to every word.

"So, Coco," Nani said as she took away my plate and handed me a gato patate. I bit through the warm sweet potato pastry of the little pasty and the syrupy insides spilled out, filling my mouth with delicious squidgy coconut. "We have nearly nine whole days to fill with mischief, just you and me!"

MISCHIEF! NAUGHTY-NAUGHTY!

Mum gave Dad a worried look, but he patted her arm. They were going to the South of

France in the morning. Mum was speaking at a museums conference and Dad was taking a week off from his work as a maths tutor and going with her to make it into a little holiday. I couldn't wait to spend time alone with Nani. She always has the best ideas for things to do, like giving each other mehndi face tattoos, tie-dying Mum's bed-sheets, or pretending to be secret agents and seeing how long we could follow strangers without them realising.

"What was that?" Mum said sharply as Nani leaned over and whispered something in my ear.

"Nani just suggested we do some gardening," I said quickly as Nani winked at me over her shoulder. I was pretty sure Mum wouldn't appreciate Nani's idea to turn the vegetable patch into a giant fishpond, but I thought it was brilliant. With ideas like that, Nani was just the person to help me find the perfect story for the competition!

"Chalo! Let's go!" Dad shouted, leaning out of the car window and honking the horn.

It was first thing on Sunday morning, and Mum and Dad were packed and ready to head off to the airport. But Mum kept running back to the house to check that Nani knew how to contact them and if she had the numbers for the doctor, the dentist, the hospital, the electrician, the plumber and the emergency services. I'm not sure what she thought we were going to be getting up to for us to need all of those people!

"Go-go-go! Allez!" Nani flapped her arms as she chased Mum back into the car. Dad blew us a kiss and accelerated down the drive before Mum could jump out again.

"Bon voyage!" called Nani. We waved them all the way down the street until they finally disappeared round the corner.

BON VOYAGE! BON VOYAGE! Cookie squawked from my shoulder.

For breakfast, Nani made eggs baked into rougaille – a spicy tomato sauce.

"Baldini time!" she announced, switching on the TV as we sat down at the kitchen table to eat. Every time Nani comes to visit we watch dozens of episodes of *Baldini Investigates*, a TV show based on a character from her favourite detective books. Baldini is a brilliant private investigator with a little triangular goatee beard, which he strokes whenever he finds a clue.

The best thing about the show is watching Nani as she watches it. She bounces in her chair shouting things like: "Liar! Don't you listen to him, Baldini! He did the murder!" or "Watch out, Baldini, she's got a gun!".

I like how Baldini always looks people straight in the eye as if he can see their secrets. He also leaves long pauses when he speaks, which made the murderous film director he was investigating in the show today talk too much and reveal her guilt. I thought that was a good tip for interviewing people so I grabbed my notebook and jotted it down – *leave long enough pauses for people to offer you extra information*.

"Bravo, Baldini!" cried Nani, thumping the arm of the sofa as the detective snapped handcuffs on to the film director and said, "I'll take it from here!"

BRAVO! squawked Cookie. I'LL TAKE IT FROM HERE! YOU'RE GOING TO JAIL, PAL!

"Even Cookie thinks Baldini is a genius," Nani said. Cookie let out one of his long cackles. "Now, what shall we do today, Coco?"

"We could make a list?" I suggested, remembering Mum telling me that when you have a guest it's polite to ask what they want to do.

We each made a list. Mine had five things on it:

Go to the seaside

Take a boat ride

Visit a museum

Go on an adventure

Find a story for the Junior Journalist competition

The last one was very important. With the deadline for entries only eight days away, I had to find my story soon!

"With a news nose like yours, I'm sure you'll find an excellent story," said Nani when I told her about the competition.

I looked at Nani's list:

Meet the king
Ride on a tram
Pierce Rani's ears
Take afternoon tea
See a famous painting!

I decided we'd do something from Nani's list first. Meeting the king would make a fantastic story for the competition, but even Nani's dazzling charm probably wouldn't be enough to get us an appointment. I put a cross next to that one. I didn't dare imagine what Mum would do if she got home to find Nani had pierced my ears so a cross went down next to that one too. I looked at the remaining things on the list and had one of my Good Ideas.

"We could do three of these in one day! Let's ride the tram to the art gallery in town.

There are lots of famous paintings to see there. Then we can have afternoon tea in their café."

Nani slapped her palm on the table and grabbed her handbag. "Chalo, Coco! What are we waiting for?"

CHAPTER TWO

A Mystery Unveiled

We left Cookie happily splashing about in some water in the kitchen sink, a thing Mum and Dad never let him do. Then we took the tram into town, while Nani crunched her way through a bag of sherbet lemons and waved merrily at everyone in the street.

I noticed people raise their eyebrows at her outfit, which I had to admit was a little unusual. Even though it was a sunny day, Nani was wearing Dad's green woolly cardigan over her bright orange and gold sari, and had his Liverpool FC scarf wrapped around her neck.

Her long plait snaked out from beneath Mum's bright-yellow hat with the pink pompom, which she'd pinned to her head with her favourite wooden hair stick with the white and yellow frangipani flower on the end. And instead of her usual sandals she was wearing thick stripy socks under Mum's glittery gold trainers. She even wore cardigans in sunny Mauritius so our spring must have felt like the arctic to her.

"Are you sure you're not too hot, Nani?" I asked, trying to ignore an annoying boy behind us who was starting to snigger.

"Hot?" cried Nani, "Coco, how you stand the icy cold here I'll never know. Now put this on before you freeze."

My cheeks were burning as Nani pulled out the frog-shaped hat an elderly neighbour had knitted for me when I was five and plonked it on my head. She'd already made me put on my winter coat before leaving the house. "There, nice and snug!"

As we passed through town, Nani pointed out a grand old building with tall stone pillars and stained-glass windows in the revolving wooden doors. "Who lives there?" she asked.

"Nobody. That's Grennards. It's a posh bank." When I was younger, Mum and Dad let me run up the steps to pat the heads of the lions that guarded the fancy entrance whenever we walked past.

"Ah, we should stop by sometime so I can change some money," said Nani, shaking her big, heavy purse which jingled with Mauritian rupees.

The tram rolled on, past the cobbled market square and the town hall with its green-tiled roof and ornate clock tower, past rows of shops and up the tree-lined hill towards the art gallery.

It was almost eleven o'clock by the time we arrived. The bright white building was made up of sweeping curves, sharp angles and colourful steps.

"Ayo!" said Nani as she stared up at the gallery. "It's like an alien spaceship!"

The gallery had already been open for an hour so I was surprised that we had to queue for ten whole minutes to get in. The couple in front of us grumbled loudly as a tall man with his hair tied up in a bun and a big camera bag over his shoulder strode to the front of the queue and was let straight in. I wondered if he was important.

While we waited, I listened in on the conversations around us and caught something about a big unveiling. *Could this be a story?* I thought, reaching into my coat pocket. My heart sank as I realised it was empty.

"I forgot my notebook!" I groaned.

"Don't worry, I have lots of paper, if you need it," said Nani, pulling a few empty paper sweet wrappers out of her bag and shaking out the sugar granules.

I smiled and politely took them, but here was a story and I was a journalist without a notebook!

The queue finally began to move and we climbed the steps into the bright entrance hall.

"We have a cloakroom if you'd like to leave your coats," said the man behind the counter, eyeing our winter clothes as he checked through our bags. "And don't forget to head to the main gallery at twelve for an exciting announcement and the unveiling of a never-before-seen collection of artworks donated to us by the late Lord Harrington."

"An exciting announcement!" I whispered to Nani as she completely ignored the suggestion that we leave our coats.

"Your news nose is twitching!" Nani laughed, as we wandered into a gallery full of paintings of serious-looking people in fancy Victorian clothes. "Who was Lord Harrington?"

"A rich man who lived in the humongous house just outside of town," I told her. "He died a few months ago. The papers are desperate to find out who he left his millions to but no one knows."

Lord Harrington had been ninety years old, but the lifelong bachelor was still whizzing around town in shiny vintage sports cars until the week he died. Last year, on his birthday, he held a big party for everyone in town with a birthday that week. My tenth was on the same day so I got to go and Mum and Dad came with me. When he'd realised he was exactly nine times my age, he'd made me the guest of honour. He'd even shown us some of the secret doors and passages in his house.

"This one leads to the throne room!" he'd said as he got Dad to lift me up to twist an antler mounted on the wall of his study.

"You have a throne?" I'd gasped as the wall swung open, revealing a wood-panelled antechamber.

"Doesn't everyone?" He pointed to a door with a gold crown painted on it and a sign which read: **THE THRONE ROOM**.

I still remember Dad and Lord Harrington roaring with laughter when I opened the door to reveal a gold-plated toilet.

Harrington Hall was amazing. It was full of all kinds of ornaments and strange stuff Lord Harrington had collected while travelling the world, as well as sculptures and paintings he'd created himself. In his will he had left the house and its contents to the town for use as a museum. As Mum managed the local museums, she and her staff had been getting the hall ready to be opened to the public.

The galleries were very hot and crowded so I was relieved when Nani finally took off her hat and scarf and let me remove my coat. The next room was more interesting than the first. On display were illustrations from an old edition of *Alice in Wonderland*. My favourite was a colourful painting of the Cheshire Cat.

"Now *this* I like." Nani stopped by an ink drawing of a fat bird with thick legs and a large beak. "The dodo! You know it only ever lived in Mauritius?"

Mum had told me that many times, but I let Nani continue, pretending I didn't know.

"It became extinct because it wasn't afraid of the first sailors to land on the island. It would waddle right up to them and before long *all* of the dodos had been gobbled up, and the rats from the ships ate their eggs. Now there isn't a single dodo left in the whole world. If only they had been as fast as they were tasty!"

As midday approached, we joined the queue forming at the huge wooden doors to the largest gallery in the centre of the building. A couple of people with press badges clipped to their coats were at the front of the line. Everyone went quiet and watched the colourful clock above the door tick away the final minutes. A loud gurgle broke the silence.

The whole queue turned to look at Nani.

"Waiting makes me hungry!" she grinned, patting her tummy.

"I could just eat a dodo sandwich!" I whispered, making her snort with laughter.

Finally, the clock struck twelve. The doors swung open and the crowd poured into a massive room filled with bizarre statues and colourful paintings. There were so many people I couldn't see anything properly, but there were lots of oohs and ahhs all around us.

"Welcome, darlings, to the first ever exhibition of Lord Harrington's life's work!" announced a woman's voice through a mic. "I'm Ms Carolyn Boyd, curator of this exhibition.

Please, sweet art lovers, prepare yourselves! For soon I will unveil our centrepiece – Lord Harrington's final painting."

I held on to Nani as she tried to squeeze through to the front of the crowd.

"Pardon. Excuse me, please," she called out. At first people acted as though they couldn't hear her then, amazingly, they began jumping out of the way. "Mersi! Thank you!" Nani said cheerfully. I followed her through the path that magically opened for us, wondering what had suddenly made everyone so polite. My hand flew to my mouth when I saw what she was doing.

"Nani!" I hissed. She had taken out her long wooden hair stick and was using the pointy end to poke anyone in her way. "Stop that!" I whispered as she jabbed a man on his bottom and he leaped aside with a yelp.

"Don't worry, Coco!" Nani booped me on the nose with the little frangipani flower decoration. "It's not very sharp. I call it my magic wand – it teaches people instant manners!"

I shook my head but couldn't help grinning as I tried to avoid eye contact with the man glaring around for the phantom bum jabber. Nani helped me up on to one of the benches in the centre of the room. At last I could see over the sea of people. Ms Boyd was standing on a small stage at the end of the room. She wore a tight black-and-white zigzag dress and lots of colourful jewellery. Her hair was white and chin length on one side, and black and shoulder length on the other. Behind her was a large painting under a velvet curtain.

"If I could have your attention, please, my chickens!" she called. A hush fell over the crowd as they craned their necks to see. She cleared her throat and spoke like a Shakespearian actor. "Beneath this curtain is the most excellent, exquisite, experimental exhibit in this entire room and the last painting Lord Harrington ever created – a very special self-portrait. A letter found attached to the back of it told us that the painting contains clues that will lead the seeker on a treasure trail to find... Well, I'll let Lord Harrington tell you himself!"

The crowd whispered excitedly as Ms Boyd pulled out a letter, propped her large purple glasses up on her nose and began to read:

Sweet puzzle lovers, gather near,
Your attention I must commandeer.
Within this painting is a clue,
To lead you to clue number two.
If you follow my puzzle trail,
You'll find a secret of great scale.
The reward for this discovery
Was once my greatest luxury.
So, look squarely at this piece of art,
Be strong of mind and brave of heart.
You have until this art show ends
To find my truth. Good luck, dear friends!

A tingle of excitement ran through me. Puzzle trails, secrets, rewards? Now *this* was a story! How could I have forgotten my notebook? Scribbling notes on sweet wrappers just didn't feel quite right.

"A secret of great scale?" called out a red-bearded man in a light blue suit. "What does that mean?"

"Yes," cried a woman in a spotty dress so bright it made my eyes hurt. "Is there actual treasure at the end of this trail?"

"And just how luxurious is the reward?" put in a man with a cap.

"Is it his missing fortune?" shouted a woman in a floral hijab.

Ms Boyd lifted her arms. "Darlings, all I know about the nature of the reward is that a cryptic note states that it is of both immense and very little value, so it's unlikely to be the so-called missing millions. What I will say is that the only thing any of us can expect from Lord Harrington is the unexpected!"

I squeezed Nani's arm as the crowd laughed and everyone began babbling among themselves.

Ms Boyd waited until the crowd fell silent. "Whichever of you dashing, daring detectives finds the final piece of Lord Harrington's puzzle must bring it here before the exhibition closes at five pm on Friday so that all may be revealed."

"That's just six days, counting today!" I whispered to Nani.

"Why such a short time?" called the bearded man in the blue suit.

"Lord Harrington left specific instructions that the treasure hunt should last only for the length of this exhibition, my lovelies," replied Ms Boyd. "And with a long-scheduled Pop Art show starting next week, alas we could only spare six days. Now, without further ado –" she grasped the curtain – "I present *The Clue*." She whisked the velvet aside like a bullfighter and the crowd surged towards the painting.

"Can you see anything?" asked Nani, standing on tiptoe. I shook my head. There were too many people crammed around it, all pushing and shoving each other, desperate to catch a glimpse. I leaped back as the red-bearded man in the suit shoved past us so roughly he nearly knocked me over in his rush to the painting.

The man with the bun was busy snapping photos of the jostling throng. As I wondered why he seemed more interested in the crowd than the painting, I heard a familiar voice above the hubbub of the crowd.

"Welcome to another episode of Steel Reveals. Don't-forget-to-like-and-subscribe. This is Lexi Steel with a thrilling reveal from the Bayley Art Gallery in Camberford." I looked over the sea of heads to spot a tall girl a couple of years older than me with pink stripes in her wavy blond hair. She was smiling into a phone camera held by a younger blond boy, who looked a bit embarrassed at the attention they were getting.

"Do you know her?" asked Nani as she heard me groan.

"Alexandra Steel," I sighed. "The boy with the camera is her brother Ollie – he's in my class." Alexandra, or Lexi as she now went by, had been the biggest personality at our school until she'd left to go to Higgerston High. She had been the lead in every school play and first to volunteer for anything that got her in front of an audience. She was loud and quite self-centred and pushy, but she was also responsible for my interest in journalism.

In Year Six she had set up a school newspaper and declared herself editor. Although she hadn't liked any of my ideas for stories, she had allowed me to help type up the articles. Sadly, the day the paper was due to be printed, everyone got called into the head teacher's office over the kind of stories we were writing. Mrs Gardiner explained that articles like **SCHOOL DINNERS: SLUGS IN YOUR SAUSAGES!**, **TOP 5 WORST TEACHERS!** and **MR MOONEY'S SECRET COFFEE ADDICTION!** were either based on guesswork, rather mean, or not at all in the public interest.

The head suggested that we write about community events or good-news stories about staff and students. Lexi thought that that sort of newspaper was far too boring and quit as editor the next day. Mrs Gardiner decided that a student-run paper might be more trouble than it was worth and so the paper was shut down before anyone even read a copy. I was disappointed, but after that I knew I wanted to be a journalist and I'd been looking out for stories ever since. Maybe if I won the Junior Journalist competition I could convince Mrs Gardiner that a school paper full of informative, true stories would be a great way for students to learn about fact checking.

"She's very confident," said Nani as she watched Lexi recording her video.

"Carol Bodd, creator of this gallery, has just made an incredible announcement about this painting by Sir Harrington."

Carolyn Boyd, curator of this gallery, I corrected Lexi in my head as she gestured dramatically towards the self-portrait. "*Lord* Harrington," I muttered between gritted teeth. She was getting everything wrong!

"A clue hidden in this picture leads to hidden treasure, terrible secrets and a HUGE reward for the finder – rumoured to be Lord Harrington's missing millions!"

"Ooh, that's not what the lady said at all!" said Nani as Lexi over-acted for the camera.

"Nope, but it makes an exciting story," I sighed. Lexi still hadn't learned anything about checking her facts. A story like this would turn everyone for miles around into treasure hunters.

While everyone was bunched up at one end of the room, Nani and I hopped down to look at the other paintings and sculptures Lord Harrington had created. Nani laughed until tears poured down her cheeks at a painting of five dogs disguised as a human. They were standing on each others' backs under an overcoat and hat, buying sausages from a butcher.

"This Harrington!" she snorted. "I like him. He had a sense of humour!"

Most of the pictures were funny. Mermaids sitting on a rock drinking cola and eating fish and chips, a bird unlocking its blue-and-white striped bird box with a huge key. My favourite was a cat dreaming of chasing tiny humans. I reached for my camera and took some pictures.

The sculptures were interesting too. Some were made from scrap metal, others from driftwood and natural objects. I smiled as I photographed a long row of heads on pedestals, each painted in dazzlingly bright colours. They were so exaggerated they looked more like gargoyles than people.

"That one looks like my neighbour Rajit," said Nani, pointing at a grumpy bright blue head with neon-pink hair. It looked half caught between a sneeze and a growl.

I giggled but the head actually reminded me more of Sir Hawxley, the man who tried to get children banned from the park that backed on to his estate. Next to that was a bust of a man with bird's nest hair, a long, beaky nose and big ears. I could swear it was based on Mayor Slater, who was currently with the rest of the crowd ogling Lord Harrington's final painting. *Were they all real people?*

Opposite was a yellow bust of a woman wearing a green tiara on her eye-wateringly orange hair. She had a gigantic nose and angry little eyes. I burst into giggles again as Nani mimicked her expression until another loud gurgle from her tummy almost drowned out my laughter.

"It's a bit early, but let's have afternoon tea now," I suggested. "We can come back and see the painting when it's quieter."

"Lead the way!" Nani shouted over her growling tum.

The café was very quiet and we got a big table in the window all to ourselves. We drank tea from fancy china cups and munched fruit scones, little sandwiches with the crusts cut off and tiny, delicious cakes. My favourites were the orange macarons that melted in my mouth.

"You're quiet," said Nani after a while.

I realised that I had been staring at the teapot for five minutes as I thought about the painting and the announcement. I had wished for an adventure and a story, and here they were.

I leaned across the table. "Nani, do you think there's any chance we could be the ones to solve the puzzle trail?"

"Any chance?" Nani slapped her palm on the table so that the cutlery bounced and clattered on our china plates. "Coco, there is *every* chance. We'll hunt down those clues better than Baldini himself and you can write our story for the competition!"

The café began to fill up. Everyone was talking excitedly about the painting. Nani and I strained our ears to listen.

"Did you see his hand?" a woman in a bright pink jumpsuit whispered to her daughter who was twisting one of her long, black braids. "His finger was pointing at a book with a rose and strawberry resting on it. I think it represents Roseberry Library."

"Did you see the map of the park on the wall behind him?" a freckle-faced boy about my age asked his older sister. "There was an X on the island in the middle of the boating lake. I bet the next clue is there!"

"There was a picture of that actress on his desk," a silver-haired lady remarked. "You know, that one from the film *Casablanca*, Ingrid Bergman. I'll bet the next clue is in Casablanca. Now where's Casablanca?"

"I think it's near Scarborough," her friend answered.

Nani's eyes shone as she listened. It was exciting to see everyone so caught up in the mystery.

"OK, Coco," she said, popping the last macaron into her mouth. "Our turn to see this painting. But first, there's something we need to get!"

CHAPTER THREE

Rolling Rupee Rumpus!

Nani bought me a cool new notebook in the shop next to the café. It had a modern art print on the cover – a multicoloured question mark.

"Perfect for my little journalist!" She grinned as I gave her a big hug.

There were still quite a few grown-ups crowded around the painting when we went back to the gallery. No one was going to give up their place as they searched for clues. The man in the blue suit was still there, so was the woman in the bright spotty dress. I jumped up and down, trying to see over their shoulders, but it was no use. How was I going to find the first clue if I couldn't even see the painting? I looked around for Nani and saw she was sneaking over to the fire alarm.

I ran to grab her hand and dragged her away.

"You'll get us thrown out!" Had Mum and Dad suspected that *I'd* be the one babysitting Nani?

I looked at the crowd and sighed. I was about to suggest coming back tomorrow when I had another Good Idea. Maybe Nani could help me distract everyone in a different way. Nani bent over as I whispered in her ear.

"Leave it to me!" she beamed.

I wriggled through the crowd. When I was as close to the painting as I could get, I raised my hand and gave Nani a thumbs up. She pulled out her bulging purse and, with a wink, tipped the entire contents on to the floor. Everyone turned at the loud jingle of rupees rolling into every corner of the room.

"Oh, my money!" Nani began scurrying around to pick up the coins. "Help an old lady, please!" she begged as she bumped into people, sending them stumbling into each other as she chased the rolling rupees. I could tell no one wanted to leave their spot at the painting as Nani crawled around the floor calling for help in a pitiful voice. Finally, a man in a striped shirt bent down to help her. Others grudgingly followed.

At last, I could see the painting. Lord Harrington stood proudly in the centre wearing a red velvet jacket over a silk floral shirt, grey hair combed back into a ponytail, blue eyes full of mischief. I immediately recognised the room as his study. I could see why so many different theories had been flying around in the café – the picture was brimming with potential clues and hidden messages. I snapped as many photos as I could, zooming in on areas that looked especially interesting – a clock with four hands and too many numbers, maps on the desk and walls, a cat wearing a crown and a jade necklace, a pile of books under Lord Harrington's right foot, the strange symbols on the rings on his fingers, the raven with a monocle perched on his shoulder.

The man with the bun appeared next to me and began snapping pictures with his big camera, which was a bit annoying as Nani had created the diversion for me, not other clue hunters. But by now most of Nani's coins had been picked up and people were starting to hurry back to the painting. I took one last photo of the entire picture and frame, then skipped over to Nani.

"You were brilliant," I said, giving her a high five.

"Hey, Rani," said a boy's voice behind me as Nani tucked her purse back into her bag.

"Hey, Ollie," I said, turning to see Lexi's brother. "This is Nani, my gran. She's over from Mauritius. Nani, this is Ollie. He's in my class."

"Ollie, ki manyer?" said Nani, kissing him on both cheeks.

Ollie went bright red and looked at me through his floppy blond fringe.

"In Mauritius people kiss on both cheeks to say hello," I told him quickly. "Ki manyer means 'how are you' in Creole. It's based on French, but a bit different."

Ollie smiled at Nani. "I'm good, thank you, Rani's nani. Nice to meet you."

"Ollie! Hurry up!" said Lexi, bursting into our conversation. "Mrs Bodd says we can interview her for another reveal. I've got a hundred views on the last one already! Come on, my viewers are waiting!"

"I was just talking to Rani and her nani," said Ollie as his sister tried to rush him away. She looked at us as though she'd only just realised we were there. Her eyes screwed up as she tried to remember where she'd seen me before.

"I'm Rani. I was two years below you at Linwood Primary," I said. Her face still looked blank. "I'm in the same class as Ollie. I've been to all of his birthday parties," I prompted. Still blank. "I worked with you on the school newspaper before it was shut down? You told me my story about the tower blocks being demolished next to the school was boring and that I should say that a secret Egyptian burial chamber had been found in the foundations?"

Lexi rolled her eyes.

"Ugh, that school paper!" she groaned. "I can't believe how boring Mrs Gardiner wanted the stories to be. She had no vision!" She sighed then looked at Nani. "Wait, you still have a nanny? Aren't you like eight, or something?"

"Ten. The same age as Ollie." I smiled through gritted teeth.

"Not that sort of nanny," muttered Ollie, his ears turning pink. "This is Rani's gran, from Mauritius."

"Oh. Hell-oh, Naaa-nee," said Lexi, over pronouncing every syllable. "Wel-come to Eng-ger-land." She waved then pointed at the ground, acting out her sentence.

"Er, thaaank yoooou," said Nani, copying Lexi's exaggerated arm motions. "Whyyy are weeee taaaaalking soooo slooowly?"

Ollie was beetroot red by now. *I'm sorry*, he mouthed at me before taking Lexi's arm and dragging her away. Nani looked at me with a raised eyebrow and a little smirk on her face.

"Sorry about that," I sighed. "I don't think she's rude on purpose, she's just, well—"

"Rude by accident?" said Nani as we watched Lexi bounce over to interrupt Ms Boyd's conversation with Mayor Slater.

I laughed as I hooked my arm into hers. "Come on. Let's go home and see what clues we can find!"

49

"You're so clever, Rani!" said Nani, watching over my shoulder as I sat at Mum's desk and transferred the images from my camera on to the old laptop Mum lets me use.

CLEVER RANI! squawked Cookie, scurrying up and down the shelf above the desk as I sent the images to the printer. CLEVER RANI! CLEVER COOKIE! PRETTY COOKIE!

"Bighead Cookie!" I said, catching a tumbler of pens as he kicked it off the shelf.

While the printer whirred away, Nani went to make some gato pima. The little chilli cakes were my favourite snack but Mum and Dad didn't make them very often.

Cookie hopped on to my shoulder as I gathered up the pictures. I brought them down to the kitchen and stuck them on the wall as Nani scooped the little golden balls from the fryer. She then whizzed some tomatoes and coriander together in the blender to make a chutney.

Nani placed a plate heaped high with gato pima on the table. I broke a steaming chilli cake in two, splodged half in the chutney and bit into it with a crunch. Nani and I munched through the pile along with chunks of warm baguette as we stared up at the photos, trying to work out the clues. Cookie amused himself by running up and down the table, whirring like the printer.

I turned to the first page of my notebook. I had already made some notes on the announcement during the tram ride home, so I would be ready to begin writing my article. Now I moved on to jotting down the ideas we had overheard in the café. None of them sounded quite right. I scanned the image from left to right, right to left and made a few more notes as I worked my way down the picture. I paused on the cat wearing the crown and the jade necklace. Could that be Kitty Royal's Chinese Takeaway? Was the next clue there? And that clock with the four hands pointing to the numbers one, four, seven and eight. Was that important?

I pulled Mum's laptop towards me, clicking off the screensaver of the long white beach fringed with palm trees in Mont Choisy, not far from Nani's village. Mum and Dad would never allow me to watch TV or videos while we ate, but Nani was very laid back. I was interested to see what Lexi had asked Ms Boyd in her interview so I searched for her video channel, Steel Reveals. The two videos she had recorded in the gallery had hundreds of views already – far more than any of her others, which were mainly about conspiracy theories or wildly exaggerated versions of local news stories. I clicked on the last video she had uploaded and Lexi's face appeared in front of the camera.

"Welcome to my second reveal from the Bayley Art Gallery where Lord Harrington's last painting has just been unveiled by curator, Carol Bodd, who is here with me now."

"It's Carolyn Boyd," I heard Ollie whisper from behind the camera as he turned the camera on to Ms Boyd. The curator gave a smile, opened her mouth to speak and was immediately interrupted by Lexi.

"What can you tell us about the treasure?"

"Oh, I called it a treasure trail," said Ms Boyd. "But that's just a manner of speaking. The letter was clear that it's a *secret* that lies at the end. I guess it's more of a puzzle path than a treasure hunt."

"Mmhmm-mmhmm," said Lexi, nodding as she faked interest in the answers to her questions. "So what is the invaluable reward for finding the last piece of the puzzle? A share of Lord Harrington's missing millions?"

"Well, we don't know what the reward is, but he said it was of both immense and very little value, so I doubt it's money—"

"What sort of terrible secrets do *you* think Lord Harrington was hiding?" interrupted Lexi.

There wasn't anything else useful in the interview, just Lexi trying to hype up the reward while quizzing Ms Boyd on information she didn't have. I wish I'd asked to interview the curator myself, I'm sure I could have asked more interesting and useful questions, but I didn't have half of Lexi's confidence. She certainly had no fear of talking to adults as if she were one herself. I had to admit I was a little bit envious.

My eyes began to water from staring at the pictures for so long without blinking. I closed the laptop, went to the fridge and poured two glasses of orange juice.

"If only Baldini were here to help us," said Nani. "What would he make of this?"

I'LL TAKE IT FROM HERE! chipped in Cookie.

I thought of Baldini's cases when he was in pursuit of his arch-nemesis Molinari, who always left a trail of false clues. Lord Harrington might not be a villain, but could he have set a trail of false clues too? I leaned back in my chair and sipped my juice. Was it all nonsense? The cat wearing a crown and a jade necklace, the raven with a monocle, the black and white picture of a film star on his desk…

"What was she called?" I asked Nani.

"Ah, that lady in the café mentioned her name," said Nani, rubbing her chin. "It's In… Ingrid. Ingrid Bergman!"

IN…INGRID! IN-GRID, iN-iN-GRID! screeched Cookie, chasing my pencil sharpener across the table.

"Shh!" I said, taking the sharpener from him. "We're trying to think."

Perhaps the clue wasn't even in the portrait itself. I ran my eye around the wooden frame, which was plain gilt with no pattern other than equally spaced raised dots all the way around. A plaque at the bottom had the name of the painting and a date engraved on it:

THE CLUE
19 18

There didn't seem anything strange about that, except for the slightly too large space between the numbers that made up the date. *Look squarely at this piece of art*, Lord Harrington's letter had said.

iN-iN-GRID, iN-iN-GRID, iN-iN-GRID! Cookie pecked at my hand, trying to get the sharpener back.

"Shush! Naughty bird," said Nani. "We can't hear ourselves think."

Then it hit me. "Wait!" I spluttered. Orange juice spilled down my chin and on to my dress as I forgot to swallow.

"Did you spot something?" asked Nani, mopping up the juice with a tea towel.

"Clever Cookie!" I scooped him up and kissed him on the beak as he made kissy noises back at me. I pulled the picture of the whole painting from the wall and laid it on the table, then ran upstairs and grabbed Mum's big ruler from her desk.

Lining the ruler up against a dot on the right-hand side of the frame and the dot opposite it on the left, I drew a line right across the painting to join them up. Moving the ruler down, I joined up each pair of parallel dots with horizontal lines then drew vertical lines to join the dots on the top and bottom of the frame until small squares criss-crossed the whole picture.

"Do you see it now?" I asked proudly.

"I'm not sure." Nani cocked her head to one side.

"Maybe this will help." Starting at the bottom left corner of the frame and moving upwards, I numbered the dots where the lines started from zero to thirty. Then across the bottom from left to right, from zero to twenty.

"It's a reference grid!" gasped Nani, leaning over my shoulder. "Like on a map. Hmm, but we don't know the co-ordinates that tell us which square to look at."

"Oh yes, we do!" I grinned. "Remember Ms Boyd said that this was the last picture Lord Harrington ever painted? So it must have been done in the last year or two. Now look at the date."

Nani peered at the printout. "1918? That can't be right!"

"Not if it's a date, but it isn't! Look at the gap, here." I tapped my finger in the middle of the numbers. The space wasn't accidental. Lord Harrington had practically told us what the numbers were by engraving the title *The Clue* right above them."

Nani's face broke out in a huge smile and she clapped her hands. "Oh, I see it. The co-ordinates were here all along! Square nineteen by eighteen is where we need to look! Bravo, Coco!"

I felt a warm glow at her praise. "Let's see what he wanted to show us." I traced one finger along the numbers at the bottom of the painting until I reached nineteen, then followed the line up to meet the horizontal line that ran from dot number eighteen. Where the lines met I drew a little cross. "X marks the spot!"

"There's nothing in that square," said Nani. "Just one of the wooden panels in the wall behind him."

"I know this room," I said. "It's Lord Harrington's study. I'll bet the next clue is in a secret compartment right here!" My smile faded, "But Harrington Hall doesn't open to visitors for nearly two weeks." With the deadline for solving the puzzle only five days away, how could we possibly get in there to find the clue? I thought about calling Mum to ask if she could arrange it, but then she might worry that we were up to something that could get us into trouble.

I slumped in my chair, looking at Lexi's smiling face on the paused video on the laptop. Would Lexi let something like an opening date get in the way of chasing a story? Of course not. Well, neither would I!

CHAPTER FOUR

The Tricky Toilet

I squeezed Nani's arm and willed the bus to travel faster. A cloud of butterflies were partying in my stomach as we drew closer to our stop. At last I saw Lord Harrington's mansion in the distance. I pointed it out to Nani and she rubbed her hands in excitement.

DING-DING! KISSES FOR COOKIE! MWAH-MWAH!

Cookie was in a screechy mood after being left at home yesterday. He'd screamed so loudly when we tried to leave that I'd had to take him with us in case our neighbour thought someone was being murdered. He wasn't behaving much better on the bus.

"Be good," I said, trying to coax him back to my shoulder as he shuffled along the back of the seat in front to get closer to the man sitting there. Cookie stared at the strands of hair the man had carefully combed across his bald spot then leaned forward and slowly opened his beak. I whisked him away just in time as he snapped at a strand of hair.

"He thinks it's a worm!" Nani giggled. Cookie wailed like a police siren in protest and the man jumped so high he almost hit the roof. Most of the passengers were glaring at us by the time the bus stopped with a hiss near the gates of Harrington Hall.

DING-DING! Cookie called merrily to all the scowling faces as we hopped off the bus. YOU'RE GOING TO JAIL, PAL! he told the driver as the doors swished closed behind us.

We headed up the sweeping, tree-lined drive to the huge, red-brick building. "It's like a castle!" said Nani, pausing to admire the round turrets and the gargoyles peering out from the neatly trimmed ivy that hugged the house.

Two stone griffins glared down at us as we walked up the steps. I could hear the radio blaring over the drilling and banging inside. My heart pounding, I stared up at the large wooden door featuring the Harrington crest – a rearing griffin on a shield.

"Are you ready?" asked Nani.

I can do this, I told myself, wiping my sweaty palms on my dress. I grabbed the tail of the dragon door knocker and hammered loudly, hoping someone would hear it over the noise.

The door finally opened to reveal a man with untidy hair, a dusty T-shirt and pale blue floral jeans. I smiled as I recognised his face. It was Tyrone, Mum's assistant. She must have left him in charge of setting up the museum.

MERRY CHRISTMAS! Cookie greeted him. Tyrone gave a puzzled frown as he looked from Cookie to Nani to me.

"Rani?" he said. "Ah, that must mean you're Mrs Ballah?" He reached out to shake

Nani's hand. "Anu has told everyone at work so much about you."

"Don't believe any of it!" Nani giggled as she grasped his shoulders and kissed him on each cheek.

"Excuse the racket," said Tyrone, nodding towards the man and woman sawing and hammering in the sawdust-strewn hall behind him. "We're creating a reception desk down here."

I realised I had edged slightly behind Nani. So, thinking about how confidently Lexi spoke to adults, I took a deep breath, stepped forward and gave him a firm handshake. The effect was slightly spoiled by Cookie hopping on to my head and pecking at one of my hair clips.

"We were wondering if we might have a little look around?" I said, brushing Cookie's red tail feathers out of my face. "I know the museum doesn't open for a couple of weeks, but Nani would love to see it before she goes home to Mauritius." It was the truth, I just didn't mention that Nani wasn't going home for five months.

Tyrone raised an eyebrow. "This isn't related to that painting, is it? The phone hasn't stopped ringing with people asking to visit since it went on show at the gallery yesterday."

My heart thudded. Had they all figured out the first clue, or were they just wanting to come here and dig around?

"Did you let anyone in?" I asked, wondering if we were already too late.

"Only… Ah, here he is now!" said Tyrone as a tall man with a bun appeared from a side door with his camera slung over his shoulder. It was the camera guy from the gallery. And he was coming out of Lord Harrington's study!

"Did you get everything you need?" Tyrone asked him.

"I think so." The man cast us a funny look as though surprised we were here. "I'll be back if not." He hurried off as though he had somewhere to be, but I was sure he snapped a few sneaky photos of us on his way out.

As Tyrone locked the door to the study, we edged our way on to the tiled floor of the entrance hall. It was bigger than I remembered. Suits of medieval and Japanese samurai armour lined the walls and a flock of beautiful Chinese kites hung from the skylight above a grand staircase that wound up to the higher floors. Five grandfather clocks each showed the time in a different country – a red and gold clock for Beijing, a clock carved with hieroglyphics for Cairo, one that looked like the clock tower that houses Big Ben for London, a Christmas-themed clock for Lapland, and a mini Chrysler Building for New York. All of their ticking and tocking competed with the hammering and drilling.

Tyrone pocketed the key and almost jumped out of his skin when he turned to find us right behind him.

I smiled and put on my most polite voice. "I know you're very busy, but could we take a little look around if we're quiet and stay out of the way?"

QUIET, COOKIE! SHUSH, COOKIE. SILLY-BILLY BIRD! said Cookie, bobbing his head at Tyrone.

"He's very well-behaved," I fibbed. "You won't even notice he's here."

Tyrone rubbed the back of his neck. "I'm afraid we can't let anyone else visit today. The hot tub on the roof sprung a leak last night. We managed to plug it, but the upstairs rooms have fragile exhibits laid out to dry and we're having to get the ceiling replastered. Why don't you come back next week?"

Next week? I looked up at Nani. We were so close to the study and now we might not even get to see if we were right about the first clue. Why was the man with the camera allowed in when we weren't? Who was he?

"Isn't there anywhere we can go?" pleaded Nani. "This may be my only chance to visit."

Tyrone scratched his head. "There's the gardens. You're welcome to spend as long as you like out there. There's lots to see – fountains, an orchard, a crazy golf course, a maze—"

"Gardens? Now look, we came here to—" Nani began.

"That would be lovely," I butted in, before she said something that might get us kicked out and reported to Mum.

The cogs in my brain spun madly as I tried to come up with a new plan. Then a crash from upstairs made us all jump.

"Argh, that's the plasterer with his ladder!" Tyrone darted for the stairs, along with the man and woman who had been building the reception desk. "I dread to think what he's broken. Drop me an email and we'll set up another time to visit."

ARGH! ARGH! ARGH! repeated Cookie.

"I've got an idea," I whispered, putting my hand on Nani's arm. "Tyrone!" I called after him. "Do you mind if I use the er…" I tried to remember the posh word Mum used for toilet when we went to restaurants. "Facilities, before we go?"

"The facilities?" He turned round and saw that I was jigging on the spot with my legs crossed. "Oh! The loo is through there." He pointed to a door. "If it's locked, Mrs Rutter the housekeeper will let you in. She's around here somewhere."

"Thank you," I called as he ran up the stairs three at a time. I waited until he was out of sight then grabbed Nani's arm. "Come on!"

"You need me to come with you?" said Nani in surprise. "I thought you could go on your own?"

My cheeks flushed as I dragged her through the door and pulled it closed before anyone heard her. We were in the little wood-panelled antechamber I remembered from my birthday visit. The wall panels to our left were covered with a bizarre display of antique toilet handles. Cookie hopped onto one shaped like a goldfish and began scratching his head against one of its fins. In front of us was the door with the gold crown on it and the sign which read: **THE THRONE ROOM**.

"Here you go," said Nani, opening the door. She whistled as she saw the golden toilet. "Ooh, how fancy! It's almost a shame to sit on it and do a—"

"I don't really need to go!" I said, quickly pushing the door closed. "When we came to Lord Harrington's birthday party, he showed us a secret door that led from his study into here. We can go through that and check out the panel."

"Bravo, Coco," said Nani. "So how do we open this door?"

I stared up at the toilet handles on the panelled wall.

"Lord Harrington pulled an antler on the study wall, but I don't know how it opens from this side? It has to be one of these handles." I pushed down on the closest one to my hand. **PLARP!** It made a loud, rude toilet noise but didn't open the hidden door. "I guess we'd better try them all."

Nani pressed another handle, which let out an even louder, ruder noise. **BLAAARt!** We both burst into giggles – proving that no matter how old you are, toilet noises are always funny. Even Cookie was cackling away, between adding to the noises. The tiny room soon rang with squelchy, burpy, farty noises as we pushed every lever. I really hoped that Tyrone and the others were still well out of earshot and didn't think the noises were coming from me. Although it might explain us being in the toilet so long.

Finally, with a big wet **BLAAAARP-PFFFFt** from a gold handle in the shape of a mermaid's tail, the whole panelled wall swung outwards revealing Lord Harrington's study. The scent of furniture polish, leather, old books and wood wafted around us as we stepped inside.

"Ooh la la," said Nani as she wandered around room, running her fingers over the huge, leather-topped desk. She raised an eyebrow at a little statue of a man with no clothes on, throwing what looked like a big Frisbee.

Cookie flew straight up to join a pair of porcelain parrots on top of a tall trophy cabinet. It was the same room as the one in *The Clue*, but contained very few of the strange items Lord Harrington had painted. He must have had great fun thinking of things to confuse people.

I snapped some pictures and pulled out my

notebook to scribble a brief description of the study in case my article needed it. I also made a quick sketch of the man who had sneaked a photo of us then drew a big question mark next to him.

"OK, Coco," said Nani, feeling her way along the wood-panelled wall. "Let's see what's behind here!"

I unfolded the picture from my notebook, held it out in front of me and counted the panels carefully. I stopped at a panel level with my forehead.

"It's this one." I tapped on the wood – it made a hollow noise as if there was a space behind it. There were no handles or antlers on the wall to twist so I tried pushing the panel, sliding it, tapping all around it. It wouldn't budge. I was getting nervous now. We'd have to be quick in case Tyrone realised we hadn't left and came looking for us.

"Let me try." Nani picked up a poker from beside the fireplace and moved to wedge it into the side of the panel.

"No!" I caught her arm and gently took the poker from her. "We've already snuck in here, imagine the trouble we'd be in if we broke anything!

"OK. No smashing." Nani looked a little disappointed. "Then how *do* we open it?"

I checked the picture again. I had drawn the grid correctly. This was definitely the right panel. I looked at the little cross I had made where the lines intersected on the picture. Maybe it wasn't just marking out the panel, maybe it was the exact spot I needed to press. I ran my finger over the wood and pressed hard where the cross was marked on the printout.

Nothing happened.

I pressed again. Still nothing. Maybe the poker wasn't such a bad idea. I stood on tiptoe and looked closer but all I could see was a tiny hole like the ones made by woodworm.

"What is it?" asked Nani, leaning over my shoulder.

"Maybe nothing. Do you have a pin, or something like that?"

Nani took out one of her earrings. "Will this do?"

"Let's find out." I took the earring, reached up and inserted its post into the tiny hole and pushed. *Click*. I grasped Nani in excitement as the panel clicked open to reveal a secret compartment. I stretched to try to peer inside, it looked empty. My smile melted. Had Camera Guy found the clue before us? Was our hunt over before it had even begun?

Nani put her hand inside and felt around in the bottom of the compartment.

"Quick, close it!" I told her as I heard a key in the door to the study.

"What are you doing in here?" shouted a shrill voice a second after Nani fumbled the panel shut. A small woman in a sensible black dress was standing in the doorway, grey hair pinned neatly back into a bun. Her hands were on her hips and she was glaring over the top of her glasses in exactly the same way my teacher does when she's about to tell the whole class off.

"Well?" she demanded.

"Nothing!" I said – my automatic reaction whenever Mum or Dad asks that question. "Sorry, I mean, Tyrone...Mr Murray said I could use the facilities, but we must have pressed some sort of secret handle and ended up here on the way out."

Nani smiled approvingly. I hadn't *actually* lied, I was just being...creative with the truth, as Mum called it. "Mr Murray works with my mum. She's in charge of Camberford's museums," I added.

"Ah, the museum." The woman's shoulders sagged. "Forty-five years I've lived here, and now my home is to be a museum." She dabbed her eyes with her apron.

"You must be Mrs Rutter!" Nani clasped the woman's hand in her own. "You poor dear. What a terrible thing to happen. Here, have a sweet." She pulled out her bag of sherbet lemons and offered them to the housekeeper.

"Er, no thank you," said Mrs Rutter as Nani steered her to a chair and handed her a tissue.

"I hope we didn't give you a fright," said Nani. "We were just admiring how clean you have kept everything. It's such a huge place. I've been thinking to myself, this Mrs Rutter – she must be a miracle worker. Just look at those gleaming trophies – a shine like that takes real dedication."

Mrs Rutter looked suspiciously at Nani as though she might be making fun of her, but Nani's eyes were wide and innocent. The housekeeper smiled. "I think I *will* have one of those sweets, Mrs...?"

"Ballah," said Nani. She pushed the whole bag into Mrs Rutter's hand. "But you can call me Sita."

"Well, Sita. It's lovely to be appreciated." The housekeeper unstuck a sherbet lemon from the bag and sighed. "You wouldn't believe how difficult it is to look after a house that has a family of ducks living in the main bathroom, a jungle of plants in the master bedroom, and more knick-knacks, curios and doodahs than anyone could dust in a lifetime."

Nani was brilliant with people. A minute earlier Mrs Rutter had been about to chase us out and now they were chatting like old friends.

"What were you looking at when I came in?" asked the housekeeper, peering at the panelled wall.

"Just admiring the lovely woodwork," said Nani smoothly. "What do you use on it, beeswax?"

"From Lord Harrington's hives," said Mrs Rutter with a nod. "I thought you might have found one of those clues that everyone's looking for. How like him to keep people amused even though he's no longer with us." She dabbed her eyes again, then almost hit the ceiling in fright as Cookie let out a gigantic, bullfrog croak. She whirled around, searching for the giant frog.

"Sorry! It's just my parrot," I said. Cookie croaked again and swept down on to the desk. He then raised his wings and squawked loudly at the window. It was my turn to jump. A large, muddy man with little twigs and leaves in his beard was staring through the glass, scowling at us from under his tattered cap.

"That's Billy, the groundskeeper," said Mrs Rutter, waving to him to go around the back of the house. "He's been working in the gardens all morning. I'd better go and see what he wants."

Billy looked from the picture of *The Clue* in my hand to the panelled wall before disappearing round the corner. How long had he been there? Had he seen us open the panel? Had he been the one to take whatever was in there?

"What a pretty bird," said Mrs Rutter as she moved to leave. Cookie was dancing proudly across the desk whistling "Happy Birthday". "He's an African grey, isn't he?"

"You know about birds?" I asked. Mrs Rutter seemed more like someone who would have a cat called Tabby or Whiskers.

"I have two little budgies – Lucky and Peaches. They don't talk to me much because they have each other to chirp to. My cat Whiskers talks to me more, in her own way." She sighed and adjusted her apron. "Unfortunately I can't take the birds with me to my new job so they need another owner. If you think of anyone who could offer them a lovely home, please let me know."

"I will," I said, feeling even sorrier for Mrs Rutter. I couldn't imagine having to give up Cookie. I wished I could take the budgies for her, but Cookie liked all the attention he could get and wouldn't put up with another bird stealing the show.

"I'd better be getting on. Lots to do and all my things to pack. It was nice to meet you both. Cookie...he won't, er, you know?"

"Oh no, don't worry," I told her. "He only poops outdoors or in his tray." *Most of the time*, I whispered to myself.

"Thank goodness. Those ducks upstairs go wherever they please and don't even ask about the monkey!"

I *really* wanted to ask about the monkey, but the housekeeper was already bustling out of the room.

"Poor lady," said Nani. "I hope she finds a home for Lucky and Peaches."

I wondered if Billy had to find another job and home too. I whistled for Cookie, who was making kissy noises at his reflection in one of the shiny trophies. He flew to my shoulder as we left the study and hurried out the front door before Tyrone realised we'd been snooping about. We wandered round the side of the mansion. We hadn't found the clue, but we could still enjoy exploring the gardens.

"I can't believe the secret compartment was empty," I sighed as Nani stopped to poke her head into an outbuilding full of tools and gardening equipment.

Nani looked around then nudged me into the work shed as Cookie swooped up to land on the roof. She pulled a slim envelope from her pocket with a grin.

"Who said it was empty, Coco?"

CHAPTER FIVE

A-Mazing Mischief!

I stared at the envelope Nani was holding, heart pounding. The words *Clue Number 2* were written on it.

"There were three envelopes at the very bottom of the compartment," said Nani. "They were all the same, so I only took one. We don't want to spoil the fun for everyone! Why don't you open it?"

I took the envelope and peered out of the work-shed door to check no other treasure hunters were in sight. I tore it open and tipped out a folded note and a gold plastic card with rounded corners. It looked like the cards used to open hotel-room doors. I turned it over, but there was no writing to tell us which hotel it belonged to. I bet it would be a super-posh one.

"A key card?" said Nani. "How exciting. What does the note say?"

I unfolded it and scanned the swirly handwriting.

Congratulations! You have found the key,
First item in a group of three.
The next, for which I beg your pardon,
Lies in the minotaur's patch in my garden.

BEG YOUR PARDON, BEG YOUR PARDON, chanted Cookie from the roof.

BLAAAAARP-PFFFFt

"Hush up, rudie!" I called to him, cringing at a flurry of the noises he'd picked up from the toilet handles on the secret door. As I made a note in my notebook – *three items to be found* – a shiver of excitement ran through me. Another puzzle to solve.

Nani laughed. "This man knew how to play!"

Cookie swooped down on to my shoulder with an almighty burp. I popped the key card into my notebook and tucked the poem into the pocket in the cover.

"To the gardens?" asked Nani.

"To the gardens!" I had one final look around the work shed as we left and deduced it must be used by Billy. It was about the size of a large garage and fitted with shelves filled with tins of paint and wood varnish, and racks of neatly stored equipment. Billy was obviously very particular about keeping his workspace neat. There was a ride-on lawn mower at the back, next to some other vehicle under a tarpaulin.

As we stepped outside, I heard a familiar chirpy voice.

"Welcome to another Steel Reveal. Here we are at Lord Harrington's former home. Viewers, the next clue to Harrington's missing millions could be right here! Don't-forget-to-like-and-subscribe for all of my exciting updates!"

"Lexi," I sighed as I peered round the corner of the house to see her standing on the steps being filmed by Ollie. He gave me a wave. Lexi grinned as she spotted us too. "I can't believe she's still going on about money!"

"Keep recording!" She beckoned to Ollie, as she hurried over to stand in front of us, giving Nani's coat and scarf a bemused look before turning to beam into the camera. "And here we have two treasure hunters!" she declared, without even asking if that's what we were doing here. "What brings you to Harrington Hall? Have you found the next clue? Or are you just hoping for a glimpse of the room of secrets?"

"Room of secrets?" Nani wrinkled her brow.

"Lord Harrington's study," said Lexi, turning away to talk into the camera again. "The room in the painting. Some say that the images aren't just clues, but point to terrible secrets. JackJay2006 commented on my last video to say that the ring on Lord Harrington's little finger has a symbol on it that when you cut it in half and mirror it, looks like an alchemist's symbol for gold. Angelteacake13 suggests that the black cat and raven could be his familiars. Was Lord Harrington a sorcerer? Could the hidden secret be his books of dark magic? Is that how he earned his missing fortune?" She whirled round to face us. "What do *you* think?"

I checked my chin to make sure my jaw wasn't on the floor. "I think… I think maybe you shouldn't listen to random people on the internet?" I blurted out. Ollie coughed loudly to cover his laughter.

"Cut!" Lexi shouted. She grabbed the phone from Ollie and swiped through the video. "Ugh, lucky this is pre-recorded," she sighed. "I'll have to edit you out. Honestly, Rani. You have no idea how to build suspense for your audience."

"Nonsense," said Nani. "Rani writes excellent stories. She'll soon have an article published in the *Camberford Herald*."

Lexi looked up. "Oh, you're entering that competition? You do know that print is dead, right? Dead boring! People want exciting stories told in an exciting way by exciting people. The only way to do that is video!"

"Even if you don't have time to check your facts first?" I asked as Ollie shot me an embarrassed half-smile. "Ms Boyd was clear the prize isn't money."

"You'll never get followers with that attitude," Lexi said as she edited us out of her video. "Right, Ollie, let's knock on the door and see if we can interview someone important."

"Later, Rani. Mrs Ramgoolam?" Ollie nodded.

"It's Ballah, but you can call me Nani," called Nani as Ollie followed his sister over to the front door.

"What a very strange girl," said Nani as we followed Cookie who had already swept ahead to the gardens. "She wants to be a reporter, yet she doesn't listen to a word anyone says."

"Or ask the right questions," I added, thinking that if she had shown any real interest in why we were there I could have introduced her to Tyrone for an interview. Though it was probably best I didn't!

The gardens behind Harrington Hall were humongous. We stopped by a fountain with a statue of a giant stone squid dragging a pirate ship down into the water and I read the last two lines of the poem again.

The next, for which I beg your pardon,
Lies in the minotaur's patch in my garden.

"What is this word?" asked Nani, pointing at the page. "Minotaur?"

"It's a creature with a man's body and a bull's head," I told Nani. Mum had a myths and legends book with a story about a minotaur. It had a picture of one that I used to flick past quickly in case it gave me nightmares.

"Ah, of course!" she said. "I know that story. It lives in a labyrinth."

"That's right," I said. "Theseus, the hero, got through it using a ball of string to help him find his way." I scratched my chin. "Didn't Tyrone say something about there being a maze here?" We stared around the gigantic garden, wondering where it could be.

"Perhaps that's it?" Nani pointed to a line of very tall bushes way off in the distance.

"I think you're right," I said as I squinted to see it. "I guess we should get walking. If Lexi is here I bet it won't be long until other people come looking for clues!"

"Wait here a minute!" Nani grinned. "I think I saw something that could help us." She scurried back towards the work shed.

Cookie flapped around me chattering excitedly, flying off to explore then returning to my shoulder before swooping away to chase the bees and butterflies flitting between brightly coloured flowers. What was Nani up to?

A minute later the work-shed door flew open and out shot a strange car with red and orange flames stencilled across the front. No, not a car – a golf cart! Nani was at the wheel, glowing with mischief. She beeped the horn as she whizzed past me, then reversed so that I could jump in next to her.

I looked around nervously. "Shouldn't we ask someone if we can borrow this?"

"Why would the key be left inside if it wasn't OK to borrow it?" said Nani, one eyebrow raised. She slammed her foot on the accelerator and we were off.

I held on tight as we whizzed across the garden, skimming over the perfect lawns, swerving around statues and narrowly missing ponds. Cookie flew after us, screeching happily. My knuckles turned white as I gripped the edges of my seat, watching through half-closed eyes. Nani was having *a lot* of fun. I really hoped Billy wouldn't see us, though he'd have been able to hear Nani from the moon!

"Whoo!" she shouted as we bounced up out of a ditch by a huge pond, setting off a chorus of angry honking from some nearby geese.

"Wahoo!" she yelled as we splooshed through a gigantic, muddy puddle beside the crazy golf course.

"Wheeee!" she squealed as we slid down a small hill which took us under a gigantic tree-house.

"Pheeeew!" I panted as we finally rolled to a stop by the tall hedges next to a massive chess set.

"I could do that all day!" Nani laughed as she patted the dashboard.

I staggered out of the cart and steadied myself against a large wooden signpost. It pointed towards a gap in the hedge:

> **The Minotaur's Maze** ⟩

This was it. I swallowed hard as I looked up at the hedge wall. The maze looked very dark and very big. What if we got lost and couldn't find our way out?

Cookie flew up on to the top of the hedge and began chatting to the other birds in all of their different whistles and chirps.

"If only he could tell us the way to the middle," I said, staring into the gloom.

"Maybe we could come back tomorrow," said Nani. "With a ball of wool like that Theseus."

"You're brilliant, Nani!" I took off the bulky cardigan she had made me wear despite the warm weather. "We *do* have some wool, thanks to you!" I picked at the cuff of one sleeve until I finally found a loose end.

"Your mum will not be happy!" said Nani as I pulled on the strand and the knitting began to unravel.

"She keeps telling me to be creative, and using my cardigan to guide us is *very* creative!" I smiled.

Nani made a tutting noise, but her eyes twinkled. I tied the strand of wool to the signpost and let the knitting unravel behind us as we headed into the labyrinth.

The maze had looked big from the outside, but inside it was ginormous! Nani took the cardigan and I tried to sketch a map of our route in my notebook as we walked. It was difficult to get the map right without knowing exactly where we were inside the maze. I kept having to rub things out every time we met a dead end and backtracked. I was very glad we had the wool to follow.

"Ayo!" cried Nani as we turned a corner to see two people with tiny bodies and giraffe necks staring at us. It took a whole terrifying second to realise it was a warped mirror that stretched us into huge heads on top of long necks. Cookie chose that moment to fly back to my shoulder then flapped away with a shriek as a huge parrot shrieked back at him from the mirror.

"I think there may be a lot of mischief in this maze," said Nani.

She was right. The maze held a surprise around every corner – more weird mirrors, a life-size mummy with its arms stretched out to grab us, a glowing skeleton that slid out of the bushes with a *wheeeeeeee*!

When the last of my cardigan unravelled I had to persuade Nani to take off Dad's Liverpool FC scarf to tie to the end of my wool.

"OK," she finally agreed. "But if I catch a cold, you must make me lots of tea."

"I will, Nani," I promised.

I could tell we were getting close to the centre now – the leafy walls were higher, the passages narrower and more shadowy, and surprises were happening more frequently. Cookie was staying way up above the hedges wolf-whistling, burping and screeching helpful comments such as: NICE CUP OF TEA! DON'T BE CHEEKY! CALL THE COPS! As I stared up at him, I could see a couple of grey clouds starting to edge across the sky.

"Enough is enough!" shouted Nani as another skeleton popped out. She swung her bag and knocked the poor ghoul's head off. "If we don't get to the centre soon, I'm going to smash my way through."

I wondered if I should be worried about Nani's love of bashing, smashing and jabbing her way through things. We needed to find the centre fast before she got us into even more trouble. I looked at my map.

"The centre has to be on the other side of this hedge, but we've been all the way around." I sighed at the thought of having to retrace our steps yet again. Then I noticed something. It was hard to see in the gloom but was the hedge a slightly brighter green here? I ran my fingers over the leaves. A large rectangle felt different from the rest – rubbery? I reached through them and felt something solid – a wooden panel.

"Why are you hugging the hedge, Coco?" asked Nani. "Let's just bash it!"

"There's no need," I said. "This whole section is fake. Give me a hand."

Nani put her hands through the leaves and together we pushed. The green rectangle swung open. It *was* a door.

MRROOOOOOWR-MRROOOOOOWR!

A deafening bellow turned my legs to jelly the second we stepped through the door. Cookie screeched up into the sky like a feathered firework. We had found the centre of the maze – and the minotaur had found us!

CHAPTER SIX

Eye-Eye!

The huge creature loomed over us. Even though it was crouched down on one knee, it was still over two metres tall with a bull's head, a shaggy human body and cloven hooves instead of feet.

MRROOOOOOWR-MRROOOOOOWR!

The minotaur bellowed again as the hedge door slammed shut behind us. I scrabbled through the leaves for a handle to pull it open. Nani hitched up her sari with one hand and waved her handbag with the other, ready to wallop the beast.

"Run for your life!" I screamed as I clawed at the hedge. But then a voice inside my head yelled even louder, *There's no such thing as a minotaur*. I stopped and turned back slowly. The minotaur hadn't moved an inch. I took a step towards it and froze as it bellowed again, exactly the same as before. *Exactly the same*, said the voice inside my head. The ice in my chest slowly melted. It was just a statue. A very real-looking statue.

Other than the minotaur and a few wooden benches around the sides, the square clearing was empty. I bent down and pulled up the square of fake grass I had stepped on to. Beneath it was a pressure pad with a wire running in the direction of the minotaur.

"If this Harrington man was still alive I would slap him. Hard!" said Nani, her hand clasped to her chest. "What if my poor heart had exploded?"

Now that the beast had stopped bellowing, Cookie flew down to perch on one of its horns and tried to copy it.

MRROOOOOOWR–MRROOOOOOWR!

"Don't you start!" I warned as I circled the minotaur. The statue was coated in skin-coloured rubber and cow hide. The horns on its head were real. So was the large leather eye patch it wore over its left eye, while the right eye was like an inky-black marble. I ran my hand over the thick hairs that ran down its back. They felt like broom bristles.

"Well, we've found the creature," said Nani. "What next?"

I stared up at the statue. Something was bothering me. I had never seen a picture of a minotaur wearing an eye patch before.

"The minotaur's *patch*! The clue wasn't talking about where it lives, but what it's wearing!" I climbed up on to the statue's bent knee, gripping its arm to pull myself closer to its snarling face.

"Careful, Rani!" called Nani as I stood on tiptoe and reached out for the eye patch. I peeled it back and screamed. Not one, not two, but *three* blue human eyes were staring out at me from the eye socket. My feet slipped and I hung from the arm as I scrabbled to regain my footing. I pulled myself back up and looked at the eyes. They were perfectly still and unblinking. I took out my pencil and gave one a wary prod. My stomach somersaulted as it dropped right out of the socket and down on to the grass.

"Got it!" called Nani. She tapped it with a fingernail. "It's glass."

I sighed with relief. But where was the next clue? I turned over the eye patch – something was written on the inside. I snapped a picture before jumping down.

I clicked on my picture of the message, zoomed in and read it out loud:

What's that? I hear you asking why,
I made three copies of my eye.
Take one, soon you'll need to use it,
Here's clue three, now please peruse it.
Seek my friend, the Dancing Deacon.
He'll take you to the oldest beacon.
Head high and there you'll see the light,
Where Bessie's voice sang through the night.

"Can I take a look at that glass eye?" I asked Nani, hoping it had never been in anybody's gooey eye socket.

I held it up to the light. It looked just like Lord Harrington's pale blue eyes, but cold and unfriendly without his kindly wrinkles around it. Why would he make copies of one of his eyes? An eye and a key card…the note in the study said that there were three items. Just one more to find. Three eyes in the minotaur, three cards behind the secret panel, Lord Harrington was very trusting to assume that whoever found each set of clues and items first wouldn't take them all to stop anyone else.

"What do you think we're supposed to do with these?" I asked, tucking the eye and the key card back into my pocket. A raindrop splatted on to my nose.

Nani glanced up at the sky. "Let's think about that back at home."

As we returned to the house in the golf cart, we heard a bellow almost as loud as the minotaur.

"My beautiful grass!" Billy leaped out from behind a topiary dragon. He was waving a rake in the air, face red with fury. "Get back here! Thugs! Hooligans!"

CALL THE COPS! CALL THE COPS! screeched Cookie from above.

"Maybe we should stop," I said, looking back at the muddy tyre tracks Nani had left in the lawn. A lump of mud smacked into the back of the cart with a squelch.

"No chance!" Nani slammed her foot down

on the accelerator and we zoomed away from the groundskeeper.

"Sorry!" I shouted back to Billy. He sent some very rude-sounding words flying after us, along with another mud ball.

By the time we got home we were drenched and covered in mud. The bus had taken ages to arrive and the rain shower had turned into a downpour. Thankfully Lexi and Ollie hadn't been around to record our escape from Billy. I grabbed some towels for poor Nani as she stood shivering and dripping in the kitchen.

"Have a warm bath," I said, draping a towel round her shoulders. Cookie copied us by pulling a tea towel over his own wet feathers. "I'll order a takeaway for dinner."

"A takeaway!" Nani let out a humongous sneeze that made Cookie flap round the counter with the tea towel still over his head like a squawky, tartan ghost. "Not while I still breathe! Check the fridge, I made a little food this morning. But change out of your wet clothes first."

I changed into my pyjamas then headed back downstairs to look in the fridge.

A little food? I thought. Every shelf was packed with plastic boxes filled with curries, dals, chutneys and sweet treats. Nani must have been up all night cooking and baking. I pulled out a bowl of biryani and put it in the microwave.

Lord Harrington's glass eye and the gold key card were sitting on the kitchen counter. I wondered what the items had to do with each other. Maybe the third and final item would reveal the connection. At least we had a head start with the first of the clues, but how long until someone else found them?

Curling up in an armchair in the corner of the kitchen, I took out my notebook and sketched the eye. I stuck the note we had found with it on to the opposite page. It was a very strange poem. I copied out the words that looked the most important, Dancing Deacon, oldest beacon, Bessie. I pulled my pencil away from Cookie who was trying to bite the rubber off the top of it. What did it mean? I drew a line from Dancing Deacon and Bessie and wrote nicknames? next to them.

I was sure I'd heard that a deacon was something like a priest. I knew what a beacon was, I'd learned about them in a history lesson. People lit fires in high places as a warning when enemies were approaching. When we had visited London, Mum told me that the flashing red lights on the top of the tallest buildings were beacons that warned planes not to fly too low. Next to oldest beacon I wrote warning light. So, we had to find the Dancing Deacon and ask him to take us to a warning light where someone called Bessie sings at night. It didn't make much sense. Maybe the beacon was the name of a theatre and Bessie was a singer there?

I thought over the puzzle as I heated the biryani and laid out some chutneys.

"Nani!" I called, dishing out the steaming chicken and rice on to two plates. The delicious smell filled the kitchen.

NAAAANEEEEEE! Cookie squawked up the stairs from the banister, mimicking my voice. PULL UP YOUR SOCKS! CHEEKY-CHEEKY!

"Coming!" Nani's footsteps padded downstairs. Her hair was twisted up in a towel and she was wearing Mum's warmest dressing gown over her fleecy pyjamas.

"Solved the next puzzle yet?" she asked as she sat down and tucked into her biryani. I shook my head and spooned some tomato and coriander chutney on to mine.

"Not really. Maybe it will make sense when we find the Dancing Deacon."

"Have you searched on the computer?"

I brought the laptop over to the dining table, taking full advantage of Mum and Dad being away, and tapped in a search for Dancing Deacon. There were lots of videos of people dancing in churches, but most were American. I didn't think Lord Harrington would want us to find someone who lived so far away. I tried a search that only looked for answers close to home, but none of the results had the two words together. I sighed and closed the laptop.

"Maybe we should go back to Harrington Hall tomorrow and ask Mrs Rutter if she knows who he is?" suggested Nani. I'd hoped we'd be able to solve the whole puzzle by ourselves, but maybe this would be the only way to find the Dancing Deacon.

Nani insisted on doing the washing-up so I spent a while searching for information on Lord Harrington himself. He was even more interesting than I had realised. There were many news stories about him, not just his missing fortune, and lots of astounding pictures.

I started making a timeline of his life, in case it would be a good addition to my article. When he was eighteen he had competed in the Olympics, winning a silver medal in men's gymnastics. He took up rally driving in his twenties and won races around the world. He climbed Everest in his thirties and wrote a book about Sherpas and their culture. His forties were spent helping to build schools and hospitals in countries that had very few. He was a playwright and poet in his fifties, took up painting and sculpture in his sixties, sailed around the world in his seventies… I stopped scrolling and stared at the photo of Lord Harrington standing proudly in front of his yacht.

"Nani, come look at this!" I called.

"What is it, Coco?" she asked, drying her hands on a tea towel as she looked over my shoulder.

"I've found it!"

I pointed out a name painted neatly on the hull of the boat:

THE DANCING DEACON

CHAPTER SEVEN

A Beacon of Hope

"The *Dancing Deacon* isn't a person," I told Nani. "It's a boat. Lord Harrington's yacht!"

"Bravo, Coco!" Nani applauded.

I read the clue again. "So the *Dancing Deacon* is a boat we need to use to get to the oldest beacon," I said, scratching my head. "A beacon at sea?"

I glanced up at Nani and we both thought of the answer at once. "A lighthouse!" we squealed. But which one?

I grabbed the laptop and searched for the oldest lighthouse in the area. There were several built in the 1800s, so I tried adding Lord Harrington's name. The answer popped up straight away. "Nani, look!" I said, turning the laptop so that she could see the newspaper article.

LOOPY LORD BUYS LIGHTHOUSE

Lord Harrington, former Olympian, rally driver, mountaineer, author, poet, artist and sailor, has purchased the derelict Signal Rock lighthouse. When we asked why, the potty peer said: "This beautiful building was the first sign of home I spotted after my long journey around the world. I want to restore it and save this piece of history for generations to come."

"This is definitely the place! Lord Harrington must have hidden the next clue at the top of the lighthouse. Now we just need to find the *Dancing Deacon*." My excitement faded a little. "Nani, do you know how to sail a boat?"

"Not a boat like that," said Nani. "When your uncle, Mamou Ved, was working on one of the tourist islands he taught me to drive his motorboat, but I don't know how these big, fancy sailboats work. Maybe we can find someone to sail it for us?"

I didn't like the idea of someone else coming to the lighthouse with us. This was *our* adventure. "Maybe," I said. "But we need to find it first."

"Mrs Rutter worked for Lord Harrington for forty-five years," said Nani. "She must know something about his boat. Let's give her a call."

Nani dialled the number for Harrington Hall and put the phone on speaker. I crossed my fingers that Mrs Rutter was still there as it rang and rang. Had she moved out already? Finally, there was a little click and we heard the housekeeper's wavery voice on the other end of the line.

"Hello? Lord Harrington's..." she paused as if unsure what to say, "former residence. Mrs Rutter speaking."

"My dear lady!" said Nani, summoning all her charm. "This is Sita Ballah, we met earlier today. I'm afraid I have a little confession to make... Your first impression was correct, we *were* there following Lord Harrington's trail of clues."

I sat on the edge of my seat, listening to Nani explain how I had solved the riddle of the painting and discovered a key card and the glass eye. She didn't mention where we had found them as that wouldn't be fair to others on the hunt. Then she told the housekeeper our theory about the next clue being at the top of the lighthouse on Signal Rock. The line went silent.

"You solved all these clues since the painting was unveiled yesterday?" said Mrs Rutter at last. "I'm...I'm impressed!"

I couldn't stop myself from jumping into the conversation. "Do you know where we can find Lord Harrington's boat, the *Dancing Deacon*? The clue said we need to use it to get to Signal Rock."

"The *Dancing Deacon*? Ah, he was very fond of that boat. He was so sad when it sank."

"Sank?" I felt my own heart sinking.

"Yes, dear. Sixteen years ago. It was hit by lightning and sank to the bottom of the harbour."

"Oh dear," said Nani. "We'd better look for another way out to the lighthouse."

"Wait!" I called out. "Mrs Rutter, you just said the boat sank sixteen years ago. Are you sure?"

"Absolutely," said the housekeeper. "It was the year of his seventy-fourth birthday."

I looked at the date on the newspaper article. "It says here that he bought the lighthouse *fifteen* years ago. These clues must have been written after that. Why would he tell us to use a boat that had sunk?"

The line went quiet again. "Wait now," she said at last. "He did buy another boat when he bought the lighthouse – a little motorboat to take him to and fro when he was working there. I wonder if that's what he meant?"

"Do you know where he kept it?" asked Nani, giving me a thumbs up.

"He had it stored away every winter but I'm sure Billy will know where it is. I'll check and call you back."

I still felt a bit wary of Billy after our run-in yesterday. I remembered his face, red with fury, as he chased after the golf cart. "Please don't tell him it's for the treasure trail!" I blurted out before Nani said goodbye.

The moment Nani ended the call, I grabbed her hands and danced around the kitchen. "A motorboat, Nani. You can drive one of those! You can take us to Signal Rock!"

"We'll see!" Nani laughed. "Let's wait to hear what Mrs Rutter has to say."

The kitchen clock showed that it was only twenty minutes until the phone rang but it felt like forever. I hopped from foot to foot as Nani spoke to the housekeeper.

"Thank you, Mrs Rutter... Oh, OK, Agnes. We'll meet you there at two."

"What did she say?" I asked impatiently as Nani put down the phone.

"Billy knows where the boat is and has

arranged for it to be brought out of storage for us."

"When? Tomorrow?" I asked.

"Slow down. It won't be until Thursday. The storage company is busy and they need to check it over first."

I could feel my face drop. That was the day before the exhibition ended. Two whole days away. Three nights! Would we be able to solve the next puzzle in time? We had solved the other clues so quickly, now the other clue-seekers would have time to find the first two items, if they hadn't already.

Then another thought struck me. What if Billy had fibbed about the delay so he could head out to the lighthouse and hunt for the final clue himself? The more I thought about it, the more I worried that he might be on the trail too. Had he seen us open the panel through the study window? Had he figured out why we were in the maze and found the eye and the clue there?

"It's not that long to wait. Before you know it, we'll be off to Signal Rock."

"Mrs Rutter didn't tell Billy, or anyone else, why we were taking the boat to lighthouse, did she?" I asked.

"I don't know, Coco. I hope not."

All we could do now was wait.

It was just as well we weren't going to Signal Rock any time soon because the next day Nani was feeling sniffly after being caught in the rain and couldn't get out of bed. Cookie perched on the headboard sniffing and coughing in sympathy as Nani spent her time drinking vanilla tea and watching old episodes of *Baldini Investigates*.

That evening, I searched for the Bollywood film I had overheard Nani singing songs from and we cuddled up to watch it with a big bowl of popcorn, while Cookie danced to the music on the headboard. By the time I went to my own bed, my head was full of songs and swirling saris.

On Wednesday, I decided to make a start on my article. But it was difficult to begin writing or even come up with a good title before I knew how my story would end. So I put all of my notes in order, along with some information I had found about Lord Harrington. I then had a go at writing the lead – the paragraph that would hook readers into reading the rest.

Lord Harrington's last painting went on display recently at the Bayley Art Gallery in Camberford. The picture – a self-portrait – was full of strange clues. An accompanying letter written by Lord Harrington said they would lead to a hidden secret and a mysterious reward for whoever finds it.

As I read over what I'd written, Lexi's voice echoed in my brain: *booooooringgggg!* I'd have to write in a much more interesting way to win the competition. Lexi might exaggerate, and even make stuff up, but she did have a way of making things sound exciting.

I sighed and checked Lexi's YouTube channel. She had a huge number of views for every video she had posted about the treasure hunt. There were seven now. A couple of them focused on conspiracy theories suggested by her viewers. In others she visited sites that might be linked to images in the painting. She had visited the island in the boating lake at the park, which I had heard the freckle-faced boy in the gallery café suggest to his sister. She'd also paid a visit to Kitty Royal's Chinese Takeaway – she must have had the same idea as me about the cat in the crown and the jade necklace. And she'd followed the Ingrid Bergman clue to the Casablanca Moroccan restaurant in town, which I hadn't thought of. She was good, even if she wasn't on the right track yet.

I clicked play on the video she'd recorded at Harrington Hall. I was relieved to see that she really had edited out her interview with me and Nani. But at the end of her video, as she poured out more exaggerated theories about what the treasure might be, I saw Nani head into the work shed behind her and come whizzing out in the golf cart.

"Well, it looks as though someone might be on to something!" Lexi said to camera as she gestured to Ollie to film me getting into the golf cart with Nani. My stomach did a little lurch as I saw Camera Guy appear from the orchard to snap a few pictures of us speeding away.

"There goes Rani Ramgoolam, from Linwood Primary School," trilled Lexi. "What did she find inside Harrington Hall? Is she chasing clues, or just off on a joyride? Stay tuned for more developments in the hunt for Lord Harrington's missing millions!"

I couldn't believe Lexi had said my full name and school on camera, and posted it online! Our teachers have told us we should *never* do that. What was she thinking? I had to get her to take down the video. I rummaged through my drawer for an old party invite from Ollie. I then grabbed the phone and dialled the number on it.

A woman answered after two rings. "Hello, Jilly Steel speaking."

Lexi's mum. I don't know why I had expected Lexi to answer.

"Er, hi, Mrs Steel," I squeaked, my anger giving way to shyness. "It's Rani Ramgoolam. Could I speak to Lexi, please?"

"Rani? Oh, from Ollie's class," said Mrs Steel. "I'm sorry, Rani, she's out with Ollie recording one of their reveal thingamajigs. Can I give her a message?"

I felt myself blushing even though I wasn't even in the same room. "Well, it's just…" I took a deep breath. "Lexi recorded me in one of her videos. She said my full name and school. I was wondering if…if she could take it down, please?"

"She did what?" Mrs Steel gave a sigh. "I am so sorry, Rani. She uploads them on my laptop so I can take it down immediately. And I'll have a strong word with her when she gets home."

I bit my lip at the thought of how Lexi would react to that.

"It's OK," I said quickly. "But thanks for taking the video down."

"Thank you for telling me about it," said

Mrs Steel. "I'll send Lexi over to apologise in person tomorrow."

"We won't be in, we're off to Signal Rock tomorrow," I said, relieved that I wouldn't have to face Lexi. As I said goodbye I kicked myself for telling her where we were going. Hopefully Mrs Steel wouldn't mention it to Lexi.

"Are you feeling sick too, Coco?" asked Nani asked as I popped in to kiss her goodnight at only seven o'clock. I shook my head. After two days of waiting, I just wanted to get to sleep early so that it could be tomorrow as fast as possible. But then I lay awake in bed until well past my usual bedtime anyway, head fizzing with thoughts about what we might find at Signal Rock.

It seemed I'd barely closed my eyes when I was woken by a shrill siren.

WAOW-WAOW-WAOW-WAOW-WAOW!

I sat bolt upright trying to make sense of the noise before realising what it was. Cookie!

I leaped out of bed as the siren echoed up from the kitchen.

"What's happening?" Nani called as I hurtled downstairs.

I switched on the kitchen lights. Cookie was running up and down the counter, wings flapping as he screeched at one of the windows. It was half open and Dad's pots of herbs had been knocked off the windowsill into the sink.

"Someone tried to break in!" I told Nani as she hurried into the room, long hair loose, eyes blinking in the bright kitchen lights.

"Stay there!" She grabbed a heavy marble rolling pin and unlocked the back door.

"Be careful," I hissed, taking a torch from a drawer. I shone it after her as she prowled round the outside of the house. I noticed that the plants below the window were flattened. Someone had been standing there. Were those footprints in the soil? Nani walked down the drive and looked up and down the street.

"No one here now," she said as she came back inside, locking the door behind us.

My legs were shaking so I flopped into the armchair. Cookie flapped over to nuzzle my ear and I stroked his beak. Who could have tried to break in? A burglar? I thought about Camera Guy snapping pictures as we whizzed across the gardens. Or had another treasure hunter seen Lexi's video and managed to track me down? What if it was Billy? Had Mrs Rutter told him about the key card and glass eye when she'd asked him about the boat?

Nani kissed the top of my head and stroked my hair as she called the police.

"What did they say?" I asked when she hung up the phone.

"They said to secure the window. They'll send someone out in the morning."

Nani locked the window and turned on the security lights, before switching on the kettle.

"It's OK, Rani," she said, handing me a mug of hot chocolate, then cutting up a peach for Cookie. "They won't be back. Cookie gave them a big fright. Didn't you, you clever bird?"

CLEVER BiRD. CLEVER BiRD, chirped Cookie, peach juice dripping down his feathers.

Nani let me into her bed for the rest of the night, but I hardly slept. I thought of how I'd told Mum we weren't up to anything each time she called. Maybe we were putting ourselves in danger by following the puzzle path. How many people thought there were millions of pounds lying at the end of the trail, thanks to Lexi's videos? Was it time to stop before we got into real trouble?

CHAPTER EIGHT

Lighthouse of Luxury

I felt a little better in the morning with normal things happening around me. The postman delivering a postcard from Mum and Dad, the sound of children playing outside, and Nani singing along to the Asian Network on the radio as she cooked up a storm.

As we waited for the police, I sat at the picnic table in the garden making a list of suspects over a pile of butterbean curry roti wraps Nani had made for breakfast.

POSSIBLE SUSPECTS:

Camera Guy

Billy

Lexi Steel

Mrs Rutter

Ms Boyd

Tyrone Murray

Other treasure hunters?

I wasn't sure about Lexi – I doubted she'd ever go as far as breaking and entering for a story. Mrs Rutter the housekeeper was also unlikely, although she did know about the clues, while Ms Boyd from the gallery and Tyrone Murray from the museum were only loosely connected to the puzzle path. But if I wanted to be a journalist, I needed to be thorough.

The police finally turned up at lunchtime. I'd expected them to roar up in vans, lights flashing, with a team of people in white coats ready to comb the house and garden for clues. Instead, we had two bored-looking officers who sat in the kitchen drinking tea, eating biscuits and barely making any notes. They didn't even try to lift fingerprints from the surfaces. I had to point out the footprints in the soil under the window, but they wouldn't pour plaster into them to make a copy, even though Nani told them Baldini would have done just that.

"I'm afraid in a case like this we're unlikely to catch whoever tried to break in," said one of the officers, brushing crumbs from his moustache. "I'm sure they won't be back, but make sure you lock up properly at night and keep using the security lights."

"Perhaps we should delay going to the lighthouse until tomorrow," said Nani after the police left. "You had quite a fright last night."

"We *have* to go today!" I cried. "Mrs Rutter will be waiting for us and tomorrow is the last day of Lord Harrington's exhibition at the gallery. Ms Boyd said the final clue must be solved before then, remember? It won't take long to get to Signal Rock. We can go straight to the lighthouse and back. Please, Nani? Pleeeeease?"

"OK," said Nani at last. "But dress warmly. I don't want you getting ill too!"

Cookie had been quite agitated all morning after his fright so I popped him into his cage in the living room to rest.

POOR COOKIE, GO TO PRISON, he said as I refilled his food and water.

"Shush, inmate." I closed the door to the cage. "We'll be back soon. Bye-bye."

BYE-BYE, RANI. HAVE A GOOD DAY, he said, mimicking Mum. **BUTTON YOUR COAT. BLOW YOUR NOSE. PULL UP YOUR SOCKS.**

It was after two when we finally arrived at the marina to meet Mrs Rutter, but Nani had called ahead to tell her what had happened so she was still waiting. Nani was wearing Mum's thick purple puffer ski jacket over a pink tunic and her gold silky trousers were tucked into fleece-lined winter boots. She had made me dig out my winter jacket and a hat with flaps that covered my ears, even though people on the beach were just wearing swimsuits. I patted my jacket pocket where I'd stashed the key card and the glass eye, just in case.

"You poor things," said Mrs Rutter, leading us down a jetty. "I can't imagine how frightened you must have been – someone trying to get into your house while you were sleeping! I've been a bit nervous at night in that big old house with Lord Harrington gone, but Lucky, Peaches and Whiskers keep me company. I don't know what I'll do without them."

I made up my mind to mention Mrs Rutter's predicament in my article. If I won the competition, maybe someone who read the *Camberford Herald* might have an amazing job and home for her.

At the end of the jetty was a red and white motorboat. Painted on the side was the name **DANCING DEACON II**. This *was* the boat Lord Harrington had wanted us to travel in! Mrs Rutter stopped dead as Nani and I were admiring the boat. She was shielding her eyes from the sun as she watched a motorboat speeding back to the marina. There was a familiar red-bearded man in sunglasses at the wheel.

"Look, it's Redbeard! Wasn't he at the gallery?" asked Nani. She was right. He was one of the people asking about the prize and had shoved us out of the way to see the painting. Was he coming from the lighthouse?

Mrs Rutter confirmed my fears. "That rude man was at Harrington Hall yesterday. Tyrone allowed him a tour of the house after he donated money to the museum conversion. He spent most of his time in the study. He left an empty compartment open in the panelled wall then headed off to the maze."

"Those are the places we found the glass eye and second clue," I burst out as my heart thunked down into my stomach. "If the compartment was empty, he must have taken both copies of the clue and keycard so no one else could get them. Did he find anything in the maze?"

"Billy went in after he'd left," said Mrs Rutter. "He doesn't like people messing up the gardens." She cast Nani a side glance but Nani's eyes were wide and innocent. "You know what he had done? He'd only stolen the minotaur's eye patch. Now why would he do a thing like that?"

My heart tumbled from my stomach to my trainers.

"Because that's where the clue was written!" Redbeard was clearly making sure no one else could stay on the trail! "Do you think he's already found the final piece of the puzzle?"

"If he has, he doesn't look very happy about it," said Nani as Redbeard tied up the motorboat alongside a row of hire boats. Hopefully she was right and he hadn't found the next clue. We might still have a chance!

"Are you sure you know how to drive this thing?" asked Mrs Rutter. She handed Nani a key. It was attached to a colourful leather key ring in the shape of a lighthouse. "Billy knows a bit about boats. I'm sure he'd take you to

Signal Rock if I asked him. I don't know why I didn't think of it before!"

I paused, wondering whether to say anything about my suspicions. "How well do you know Billy?" I asked.

"Very well, dear. He has worked at the hall for nearly twenty-five years."

"And you trust him?"

Mrs Rutter thought for a moment. "He's trustworthy enough, although I wouldn't trust him around my pets. I once saw him spray poor Whiskers with the garden hose. All she was doing was, er, helping him fertilize his rose bushes."

Nani looked at me, one eyebrow raised.

"She pooped in his plants," I whispered.

"Why are you asking about Billy?" said Mrs Rutter.

"Just wondering," I replied, deciding not to scare her with my theory that he might have tried to break into our house last night.

"No need to trouble Billy," said Nani, climbing down into the boat and taking the wheel. "I'm looking forward to ripping through the waves in it myself."

I gave Mrs Rutter what I hoped was a reassuring smile as Nani rolled up her sleeves.

The *Dancing Deacon* really was a lovely boat. It had soft red leather seats and a roof that could be rolled back so we could feel the sea spray on our faces. Nani even let me take a turn at the wheel once we were out of the marina. It wasn't a fast boat, but it was still exciting to steer and it made a funny little *put-put-put* noise as though singing to itself.

Nani took back the wheel as we drew closer to the lighthouse on Signal Rock, which rose majestically from the sea towards the vast blue skies. I reached for my camera and took a couple of pictures.

"Can't we go any faster?" I said, checking my watch. It was already after three and we needed to get back before it got dark.

"I'm trying," said Nani, "but I think the boat is getting tired."

The engine did sound weaker than when we had set out. The *put-put-puts* were starting to sound like little gasps.

"The exercise must be a bit much for the poor thing after so long stuck in a boat shed!" said Nani. She gave the wheel a pat as she cut the engine to drift alongside the jetty.

I clambered up on to the wooden platform and Nani passed me the mooring rope. Once I'd tied it to an iron ring set into one of the rocks, I held out my arm to help her from the boat.

"It's amazing!" I stared up at the postcard-perfect blue-and-white striped tower looming over us. Seagulls launched themselves from the top and sailed overhead, shrieking at us for invading their home. The little rocky island was pitted with rock pools and draped with seaweed where it was covered by water at high tide.

I held Nani's arm as we climbed the rough, seaweedy steps up to the door. But when I rattled the handle, it was locked. I hadn't even thought that the lighthouse might be locked. How were we supposed to get in? I checked the key card in my pocket, but I couldn't see anything for it to be swiped against.

"We could smash the lock with a rock?" Nani suggested as she looked around for a good heavy one.

"No smashing," I said firmly. Besides, the lock and metal door looked secure enough to withstand a battering ram. I sat on one of the rocks with my chin in my hands. Why would Lord Harrington send us out here knowing the lighthouse would be locked?

"I don't suppose the key was with the boat key?" I asked Nani, even though I already knew the answer.

"No, just one key," said Nani, handing it to me.

The only other thing on the key ring was the leather tag. It looked exactly like the lighthouse standing before us – the same blue and white stripes, the same number of windows and the same large blue door with the date the lighthouse was built carved into the stone above it: 1847. The tag even had that date, in tiny writing.

I turned the tag over in my hand. Could this be the clue? Lord Harrington had been very clear that we needed to use the *Dancing Deacon*. Maybe that gave us an advantage over Redbeard? I walked round to the back of the lighthouse – if a circular building could have a back.

"Careful, Rani!" Nani called after me. "Those rocks are slippery!"

The main details of the back of the lighthouse matched the reverse of the tag too – the same number of windows, the drainage pipe running down the side. Then I saw it. A tiny cross scratched into the leather, on the blue strip near the base. I wondered if it was just an accidental mark, but it looked like a carefully drawn "X".

I looked for the same point on the lighthouse itself and realised it did mark something out – a little blue-and-white painted bird box. I had a feeling I'd seen one like it recently, but where? Harrington Hall? In *The Clue* painting in the gallery?

I flicked back through the photos on my camera and came across the picture I'd taken of a painting in the gallery – a bird unlocking its home with a great big key. Lord Harrington had left a clue in that painting – the key to the lighthouse was in the bird box!

Unfortunately, there was an angry-looking seagull perched right on top of it, glaring straight at me.

"Gooood birdie, niiiice birdie," I mumbled as I crept towards the bird box, hands held out in front of me. The gull glared down its sharp yellow beak and raised its wings threateningly. I hadn't realised quite how big seagulls were. I reached slowly into my pocket for the gloves Nani had made me bring. I doubted they'd do much against that beak, but any protection would do.

As I pulled out the gloves, something wrapped in greaseproof paper fell from my pocket – a roti wrap left over from breakfast. As the seagull launched itself towards me, I snatched up the wrap and hurled it across the rocks. The gull's wingtips brushed the top of my head as it wheeled towards the food, screeching at four other gulls who swept down to squabble over it.

"Ugh. Sky rats!" said Nani as she hurried over to see what the noise was. "Did you find something?"

"Maybe." I took a deep breath and poked my fingers inside the bird box, feeling around until I touched something metal at the bottom. I hooked it out and turned back to Nani.

"Bravo, Coco!" she cheered as she saw the large iron key in my hand. "Now open up quick, before my ears freeze off!"

The lock was stiff so I had to grasp the key with both hands and force it to turn. The door swung open into a big, round room, which made up most of the ground floor. It was lit by four round windows that let light flood in from all directions.

"This must be where Lord Harrington created his artwork," I said as we walked between half-finished sculptures and paintings. Several large sacks sat by the stairs leaking white powder across the floor.

"What is this?" asked Nani, one eyebrow raised in suspicion. I leaned down and brushed white dust from one of the sacks to reveal the label: **PLASTER OF PARIS**.

"It's just plaster," I said.

As I stood up again, I came face to face with a grotesque head. "Argh!" I yelped, jumping back.

A whole row of detailed, snooty-looking heads stared out at us, sitting on a long, curved shelf. They were carved from wood and seemed familiar.

"What are those funny things?" said Nani.

"They're like the heads from the Lord Harrington's exhibition," I said, reaching up to touch the nearest one. It toppled over and rolled off the shelf to be caught by Nani.

"So light!" she said, tossing it to me.

"I think it's balsa wood." I turned the head over in my hands, before popping it back on the shelf. "We've used it in school. It's quite easy to carve." I noticed a box of rubber moulds in a box by the plaster sack and pulled a couple out. "He must have carved the wooden heads to make moulds for the plaster heads on display at the gallery." I dropped the moulds back into the box, wondering why he didn't just put the wooden heads on display instead of casting them in plaster. Nani was poking around the room again, running her hands over the brushes, tubes of paint and canvases spread over every surface.

Lord Harrington had even used the walls as a canvas, covering them with coral reefs, gardens of anemones, strange, colourful fish, mer-people, and many-tentacled sea creatures. It was like being in a bizarre aquarium. A staircase followed the curved wall up to the next floor and I remembered the words from the last clue. *Head high and then you'll see the light.*

"Come on!" I called as I made my way to the stairs.

"Go ahead," Nani's muffled voice called from a cupboard. "I'll take my time."

I left Nani happily exploring and dashed upstairs to the next room. It was a kitchen with a little stove, a sink and a curved table next to a window that looked out to sea.

The next floor was a library, with a thick carpet, cosy armchairs and hundreds of books filling the curved shelves running around the walls. There was even a ladder on wheels to reach the top shelves where there was a whole section dedicated to astronomy and cosmology. Under the window was a squishy sofa with lots of cushions. I wanted to throw myself on it with a pile of books, but there was a puzzle to solve and treasure to find.

The door at the top of the next flight of stairs led into a bedroom with a large four-poster bed, more like something I'd expect to see in a fancy hotel than an old lighthouse. The staircase was enclosed by walls at this point so that people going upstairs wouldn't be walking through the bedroom.

Finally, I reached the top and emerged in a beautiful bright room with windows for walls, the diamond-shaped panes tinted different bright colours. I spun around in the rainbow that danced through the room. In the centre was a circular lamp chamber from which a light once shone brightly to warn ships they were close to the rocks. There was no lamp in it now. It was sealed shut – just a backdrop to a curved sofa which had been built around it so that you could sit and gaze out in any direction.

So I had reached the light – now what?

I looked under the sofa and behind all of the cushions. Nothing. Finally I flopped on to the sofa and made a few notes in my book then watched the seabirds soaring outside as I waited for Nani to finish exploring. Considering there were so many books on astronomy in the library, I was surprised Lord Harrington hadn't installed a telescope up here.

"Ayo!" Nani cried as she climbed up into the lamp room and plonked herself down next to me. "Zoli! Beautiful! What a view."

A tern landed on the balcony and tapped its beak on the window, peering in at us with beady little eyes as if expecting something.

"I bet Lord Harrington used to feed them." I got up and opened the door. The bird flapped away then circled back to land on the railing, watching as I stepped on to the metal balcony. Was the clue out here?

"Careful!" called Nani. "It might not be safe."

"It's fine." I jumped up and down to show how solid it was. "Come and see."

Nani covered her eyes. "I'll stay here, thank you."

I'd forgotten Nani was afraid of heights. I wasn't, but when I looked down to where the waves crashed on the rocks far below, my stomach did a little flip. I turned into the wind, enjoying the feel of it blowing back my hair. I then put my hands on the railing and stared into the sky.

"OK, Lord Harrington!" I shouted into the wind. "We're here! What next?"

CHAPTER NINE

All at Sea

The wind whipped my hair into my face as I gripped the top rail of the balcony and carefully made my way around the lighthouse, searching for the next clue. Nani watched from inside the lamp room, eyes half covered.

The only thing out there was a large brass bell hanging from a frame. It must have sung out to warn ships when they were close to the rocks. There was nothing remarkable about it, other than it appearing to be a favourite perch of the terns as it was splashed with white droppings.

Nani gave a sigh of relief as I came back inside. "Any luck, Coco?"

I shook my head. Nani was reading Lord Harrington's letter again. I sat down beside her and read it over her shoulder.

"*Head high and then you'll see the light, where Bessie's voice sang through the night.* Well, here we are," I said. "But what are we looking for? Maybe something inside the light?"

I leaned on the back of the sofa and peered through the huge lenses that would have magnified the bulb inside. There wasn't even a bulb there now, the lamp chamber was completely empty.

"Could Bessie have been the lighthouse keeper?" asked Nani. "Do you think she sang in here?"

I looked around but nothing in the room suggested someone might have sung from a particular spot.

The light was changing outside. The blue sky was now streaked with orange giving everything a golden glow.

"We should get back before it gets dark," said Nani. "We can think about this at home and come back first thing in the morning." I nodded. Cookie would be waiting for us and I didn't like the idea of being around if the bearded man decided to return. After last night I was worried that some treasure hunters might go to desperate lengths to get to the prize.

"Another night to wait," I groaned as we made our way downstairs.

"Don't think of it like that," said Nani as we stepped out into the salty sea air and locked the lighthouse door behind us. "Think of it as more time to enjoy Rani and Nani's great journey down the puzzle path!"

"Maybe that should be the title of my article," I smiled. We walked down the little jetty and helped each other down into the *Dancing Deacon*. Nani's smile faded as she turned the key. The engine coughed, spluttered, then went completely silent.

"What's wrong?" I asked as she turned the key again, and again, then tapped a little dial.

"It needs fuel. I should have checked before we set out, but I was sure it would have been filled for us. Not to worry, I'm sure there'll be some here somewhere. Could you look for it?"

Nani was trying not to sound anxious, but her lips were a tight, thin line as she tried to start the boat again. I looked inside every compartment I could see, but all I found were lifejackets and ropes. Not even a flare to signal that we were in trouble.

"I'll check the lighthouse." I grabbed the key and hurried back up the steps. Lord Harrington *must* have stored some petrol here to refuel the boat. I threw open every cupboard in the studio, searching behind cans of paint, piles of canvases, old brushes and broken pieces of plaster.

There was no fuel to be found.

"Don't panic," said Nani when I told her the news. She took out her phone. "I'll call Mrs Rutter before we bother the coastguard. She can send the people who stored the boat to help us." She rang the number, held the phone to her ear, then shook her head. I took one look at the little symbol at the top of the screen and knew it was no use trying.

"There's no signal." I thought fast as I tried to stay calm. We were in a lighthouse, built for sending signals, on an island called Signal Rock, but with no way of signalling land. We headed up to the lamp room and I checked the phone again. Still no signal, even from up here. Nani sank into the sofa as I paced the room. How could we let people know we were here?

"Is there something to use to make a really loud noise?" asked Nani. "I saw a gramophone in the library."

I shook my head, the sound would be lost on the wind. Then it struck me. The bell outside had once sung out to warn ships away from the rocks, maybe it could help us too.

"Careful, Rani!" Nani shouted as I stepped out on to the balcony and made my way round to the old bell. I picked up the end of rope attached to the bell's clapper and gave it a pull.

I expected it to be very loud but instead it made a disappointingly muffled clunk.

I stared at it in surprise and beneath the tern droppings I noticed a little plaque welded to it. I scrubbed at the droppings with the end of the bell's rope and gasped at the letters revealed:

OLD BESS

Bess! Was this Bessie? A bell would have sung warnings to ships on foggy nights. I reached inside the bell and laughed out loud as my fingers brushed against a package. Then another, three in total. We *were* the first to find Bessie! My heart pounded as I pulled out one of the packages and dashed back inside.

"I found it!" I cried, closing the door against the wind. "Bessie is a bell!"

"Of course!" said Nani as I sat on the floor and ripped the package open, all thoughts of signalling land forgotten. Inside was a thick cream envelope addressed: *To the Great Adventurer.*

"That's you!" Nani squatted down next to me as I opened it to find a letter and yet another envelope. On the front were the words: *You are not the one for whom I'm intended. Open me and your quest is ended.* On the back was a wax seal with a griffin stamped into it – Lord Harrington's family crest.

"I wonder what's inside," said Nani, holding the sealed envelope up to the light.

"Don't open it!" I warned her. "It's not for us." I smoothed out the letter that had been with the mysterious envelope. It had the same crest printed at the top:

Daring detective, new-found friend,
Your search is nearly at its end.
You broke my codes and found the letter,
Baldini couldn't have done better!

153

"He watched Baldini!" Nani squealed. "Sorry, Coco. Go on."

Visit the vault guarded by lions,
Give the envelope to Orion.
The card and eye used in succession,
Will serve up my most dire confession.
Take it to my exhibition,
The venue for my great admission.

One last riddle to solve! "I guess Orion must be a person," I said, thinking aloud. "But why would they be in a vault?"

"A vault?" said Nani. "You mean...a tomb?"

I shivered. Surely the last piece of the puzzle wasn't hidden in a grave?

"That can't be it," I said. "A vault is also where you store things...like a cellar." I couldn't imagine anyone keeping a lion in their cellar though, even Lord Harrington.

"Perhaps he means a safe," suggested Nani. "Like in a bank?"

My mind whirred. It made sense, but what

kind of bank would have lions guarding it? I chewed my thumbnail as I thought, earning a frown from Nani who always had neat, shiny nails. An image of a building crept into my head. A building we had seen recently. One with two stone lions guarding the entrance.

"Grennards! The bank you pointed out from the tram. That *must* be it, Nani! You. Are. Brilliant!" I kissed the top of her head.

"Mersi." Nani smiled and patted her hair. "Of course, I already know."

I slumped back against the back of the sofa. In the heat of the discovery I had almost forgotten we were stuck here.

"We have all the items, we know where to take them, but we have to solve the next puzzle before the gallery closes at five tomorrow. Who knows how long it will be before we are rescued!"

"Coco!" Nani took my hand and squeezed it. "Whether we make it in time or not, we've still had a wonderful adventure. And you have a story to tell."

I smiled and squeezed her back. One of the things I loved so much about Nani was her ability to see the good in any person or situation. She was right, but I could tell that she was worried beneath the smile. I looked out of the windows. Maybe Bessie could also help us get back to land today.

I headed out on to the balcony and carefully removed the other two packages from inside the bell. I pulled on the rope and this time she sang out with a deep tone so loud my ears rang too. I pulled my hair and hat over them and kept on pulling.

DING-DING, DING-DING, DING-DING!

Up here the sound was almost deafening, but the boats in the distance seemed too far away to hear and the wind swept the noise away. At one point I thought that a small yacht might be heading towards us. I shouted and waved, but it veered off towards the marina as if the crew couldn't hear a thing. The bell must have been a final warning when sailors were already close to the rocks.

I kept on anyway. Bessie sang, and sang, and sang as the sun sank into the horizon, casting an orange glow over the sea as the evening chill set in.

Eventually, I became aware of shouting behind me. Nani was edging shakily round the balcony. She grasped the rope and pulled it gently from my hands to stop the bell ringing.

"Stop! Please, Coco." She touched her hand to my cheek. "It was a good idea, but there won't be many boats heading this way now. Come back in. Let's light a fire and put our heads together."

My ears were still ringing as I taped the packages back inside the bell for other clue seekers, then took Nani's arm to lead her back inside. Her eyes were rolled up towards the sky and her teeth chattered with cold and fear.

"Sorry, Nani." I grabbed a blanket from the sofa and wrapped it around her shoulders.

"We should go down to the kitchen and warm up. I'm sure we'll think of something."

But as dark shadows crept through the lighthouse, I knew the truth. We were trapped.

CHAPTER TEN

HELP!

Nani lit the log burner in the kitchen and the warmth gradually made its way through the room. Shadows danced across the walls as she disappeared down the spiral stairs to the studio. There was a loud *clunk* and suddenly the light bulbs flickered to life. The fridge in the corner began to whir and a little red light went on above a switch by the cooker.

"That's better," said Nani as she came back up the stairs. "I thought I saw a generator down there. Now I can make a nice cup of tea."

I couldn't help but grin as she reached into her handbag and pulled out a Tupperware box full of samosas, roti wraps and a packet of vanilla teabags. She was always prepared for an emergency – so long as the emergency was an empty stomach. Soon we were sitting on a rug in front of the roaring fire, munching on our snacks and sipping vanilla tea. Nani had sweetened it with a tin of condensed milk she had found in a cupboard, just the way we drank it at her house in Mauritius, sitting on the veranda watching the rain dripping from the coconut palms.

"There's enough canned food here to last for days," said Nani, checking through the cupboards. But I could tell she was nervous from the way she was twisting the bottom of her long plait.

"Mrs Rutter wanted us to call when we got back," I said as brightly as I could. "I'll bet when she doesn't hear from us by tomorrow morning she'll send someone out. You'll see." I just hoped that someone wouldn't be Billy. Could he have been responsible for the boat running out of petrol, or was I just being paranoid?

After dinner we curled up in the comfy armchairs in the library. I clipped the letter from Lord Harrington into my notebook as Nani played records on the gramophone. What could the "dire confession" from the last line of the clue be? I hoped it wasn't anything too awful.

"Isn't it beautiful!" said Nani, head tilted and eyes closed as she listened to a woman's voice crackling out of the gramophone horn. "Much better than your digital music."

I had no idea what she was talking about. At least the music I listened to didn't sound all crackly.

I'd left the mysterious letter for Orion in the lamp room so I popped back up to fetch it. I felt around for a light switch and touched a cord hanging from the ceiling. I gave it a pull, but instead of turning on the light, a large hatch opened up. A dull red glow was coming from inside.

"Nani!" I squeaked, backing towards the stairs, half afraid a cloud of bats would come spiralling out like in a scary movie.

"What is it, Coco?" she called, making her way up with a torch from the library. She pointed the beam up at the hatch and I saw a wooden ladder neatly folded into it.

"What could be up there?" she said as she passed me the torch and folded down the ladder.

I gulped as I remembered how Lexi's viewers had claimed that Lord Harrington might have been a sorcerer. It had sounded silly at the time, but the creepy red glow made me even more nervous about what his confession could be. Was there some terrible secret up there?

Nani climbed the ladder, clinging tight to each rung despite the ceiling being quite low. "Ayo!" she exclaimed as she poked her head through the hatch. "Come quick!" She sounded too excited to have seen something scary so I followed her up the ladder.

At the top was a large, softly lit dome.

A big, metal cylindrical instrument stood in the middle of the room. A telescope.

"It's an observatory!" I gasped. No wonder Lord Harrington hadn't put a telescope in the lamp room – there was a giant one just above it.

Nani turned a metal wheel on the wall and the dome above us split in two to reveal a perfect slice of night sky. Stars glittered above us like diamonds in black velvet. What a perfect place for an observatory. Out here, far from the light pollution of town, there were more stars than I had ever imagined.

With a bit of experimentation, we managed to get the telescope working. On a side table we found a handmade guide in Lord Harrington's swirly handwriting. We followed the instructions and were soon admiring the huge craters on the surface of the moon.

"Look here!" Nani stepped aside after adjusting the telescope to co-ordinates and magnification documented in the guide. "I've found Jupiter!"

I stared in amazement at the gas giant. "I can

see its red spot! My teacher, Ms Moore, said that it's a giant storm, more than twice the size of Earth. I can't believe I'm looking at the real thing! Imagine if there was an astronomer here who could show us where to find all of the planets in the solar system and even other galaxies."

Nani placed her arm round my shoulder. "If only everyone could have the opportunity to see the skies like this."

Finally, we made our way down to bed, heads full of stars. Nani lit a little lamp on the table as we got into the soft four-poster bed.

"Do you think Cookie will be OK on his own?" I asked.

"He'll be just fine," said Nani. "You left him lots to eat and drink and he has his toys to play with. I bet he's not even missing us yet."

I wasn't sure about that, but I chose to believe it as I snuggled down under the quilt. Before long the only sounds were Nani's rumbling snores blending into the gentle roar of the sea.

I opened my eyes to see the morning sun creeping across an unfamiliar ceiling painted with blue sky and clouds. Nani's side of the bed was empty and food smells were drifting up the stairs.

I looked out through one of the round windows as I got dressed. Gulls and terns drifted in the endless sky over the sparkling sea. If we weren't trapped, I would have been happy to stay here forever, watching the birds and sea by day, the universe by night. I wondered what would happen to the lighthouse now Lord Harrington was gone.

"Good morning, sleepyhead," said Nani, placing a bowl in front of me as I sat down at the kitchen table for breakfast.

"Wow, beans and veggie sausages!" I tucked straight in, then started hiccupping as the chilli flakes Nani had added caught me by surprise.

"We're lucky there's enough tins in these cupboards to last a month!" said Nani. "Oh, don't worry," she added as my face dropped. "We won't be here that long. Let's go back up to the top after breakfast. We could try ringing Bessie again."

We shared a tin of pineapple chunks in the lamp room as we kept a look out for any boats heading our way.

"I miss my toothbrush," I said after drinking the remaining juice straight from the tin.

"Try this," said Nani, pulling a packet of sugar-free gum from her bag and handing me a piece.

We took it in turns to keep watch, but by lunchtime I was worried. Even worse, I could tell Nani was too. What if we were still here when Mum and Dad came home? Would the clues on the kitchen wall lead them to us? That was days away, though. What would happen to Cookie?

Nani went down to make lunch while I sat on the balcony, legs dangling over the edge, arms and chin resting on the lower railing. My eyes watered in the wind as I willed the boats in the distance to come our way. If only there was a way to sign to them that we needed help. A sign – that was it!

My left leg prickled with pins and needles as I scrambled to my feet. I hopped back through the lamp room and down the stairs towards the bedroom.

"Is everything OK?" called Nani as I hurtled through the kitchen and down the next flight of stairs, dragging the white bed-sheet behind me.

"Fine!" I called back. I spread the sheet out on the floor then went to gather up some paints and brushes.

"Oh, Rani!" cried Nani as she came down a few minutes later to tell me lunch was ready. "What are you doing to that lovely cotton?"

There had only been enough paint in each tube for one large letter, so I'd used bright fuchsia, turquoise, plum and marmalade.

"Now why didn't I think of that?" said Nani, hands on her hips as she looked at the huge, colourful letters I had painted on the sheet:

HELP!

"It's acrylic paint," I said. "It dries quickly, but we'd better leave it a little while so it doesn't get all smudgy when we take it upstairs."

After a lunch of tinned potatoes fried up with tomatoes and spices, we carried the banner up to the lamp room and tied it to the balcony railings on the side facing the marina. Even if it wasn't quite readable from there, we hoped a passing boat might read it. Nani kept her eyes half closed as she tied her corner. I didn't like asking her to come out here, but I could barely hang on to the sheet as it flapped in the breeze and was afraid it would carry me away into the clouds like a giant sail.

At last the banner hung in place, fluttering our cry for help. I had tied stones to the two bottom corners so that the sheet didn't blow about too much. Nani made some tea and we sat down on the sofa in the lamp room to wait.

After about an hour I finally spotted something – a speedboat, bouncing across the water towards us!

"Someone's coming!" I shouted so loudly that Nani dropped her biscuit into her third cup of tea. I shaded my eyes with my hand and squinted out at the boat.

"There a man driving it," I called. "Billy! There's someone with him. It's… It's Mrs Rutter!

You were right – she must have been worried about us!" I was even happy to see Billy.

"Quick, help me!" Nani jumped up and grabbed our mugs.

"What is it?"

"We can't let them see the place in such a mess!"

"Nani, they're rescuing us, not coming for afternoon tea." I shook my head as I followed her downstairs to help make the bed and tidy the kitchen.

Ten minutes later we were standing on the jetty, waving as the speedboat cut its engine and glided in to bob gently behind the *Dancing Deacon*. Billy grunted a grumpy greeting. I guessed he was still angry with Nani for tearing up his lawn. He had one of those strange faces that didn't often change expression. Detective Baldini would call him difficult to read.

Mrs Rutter clambered unsteadily out of the boat to meet us.

"Oh, Agnes, we're so happy to see you!" said Nani, grabbing Mrs Rutter and kissing her on both cheeks. "We ran out of fuel and thought we'd be trapped for days."

"I didn't hear from you yesterday so I called the marina this morning to check that you'd returned the boat," said the housekeeper. "When the marina manager told me you hadn't, I came straight down to ask around. And that's when I saw your sign hanging from the lighthouse. I called Billy and he borrowed a boat to bring us right out here instead of bothering the coastguard. Wasn't that good of him?"

"Thank you, Billy," said Nani.

"Did you find what you were looking for?" Mrs Rutter whispered to us as Billy untied the *Dancing Deacon*'s mooring rope and secured it to the back of his boat.

"Yes," I said quietly. "Another riddle. It was inside the bell."

"Another one? And have you figured out the answer?"

"Part of it. We need to go into town to find a final piece of the puzzle." I didn't want to reveal exactly where it had directed us to in front of Billy. "We'll need to use the items we've found."

"And you have them with you?"

I nodded, closing my hand tightly round the glass eye and key card in my pocket.

Mrs Rutter turned to Billy. "Right! Let's get these ladies back to land. They're on a special mission and every second counts!"

CHAPTER ELEVEN

Orion's Lions

Billy revved the motor and we were off, flying over the water. The salty wind blew back my hair and stole the breath right out of my nose. The speedboat was much faster than Lord Harrington's, but not nearly as interesting.

"The *Deacon* really is dancing now," I said to Nani as we watched the little boat skipping over the waves behind us. I looked back at the lighthouse. My sign looked smaller and smaller as we headed for land. I was impressed that Mrs Rutter had managed to read it from the marina.

"Here, have something to drink," said the housekeeper, handing us small cartons of apple juice from her bag. As I took one I noticed that her arms were bandaged beneath her cardigan.

"Did you hurt yourself?" I asked.

"Nothing serious." She smiled. "I lost a fight with a feather duster!"

We were back at the marina in only twenty minutes, twice as fast as our trip out to the lighthouse.

"Quickly now!" Mrs Rutter hurried us out of the boat as Billy moored the *Dancing Deacon*.

I wondered if he ever smiled or said more than two words. Though maybe I was being unfair. We had made a mess of his lawn and yet he had still come to our rescue. "Thanks again for coming to get us!" I called.

He gave a small nod, then got back to his knots.

"Do you know where we can get a tram to Grennards?" Nani asked Mrs Rutter as she herded us along the jetty.

"Grennards?" said Mrs Rutter, eyes wide.

"So that's where the final piece of the puzzle is? How about I drive you straight to town?"

As we weaved through the holidaymakers on the boardwalk, I spotted Redbeard getting into a boat. This time he was with a man carrying a large toolbox. Were they going back to the lighthouse to try and break the lock?

I heard a clicking behind us and looked over my shoulder to see Camera Guy snapping photos of us. I'd had enough. Why was he everywhere we went? I stopped and whirled round, about to confront him, when the last voice I wanted to hear right then broke through the hubbub of the crowd.

"Welcome back to this exciting Steel Reveal. Don't-forget-to-like-and-subscribe. Here we have the treasure hunters, fresh from their dramatic rescue!"

Lexi Steel. Ollie was with her, but Lexi was filming us herself with a selfie stick now. Probably because Ollie was too embarrassed to film for her.

I covered my face with my hand as she walked in front of us, angling the camera to keep us all in frame. "Tell us, how did you get trapped out on Signal Island? What did you find there?"

Signal Rock. My inner voice corrected Lexi.

"Oh, we found something very exciting," said Nani before I could stop her.

"Shh!" I hissed. If Nani told Lexi what we had found or where we were going it would be online in minutes.

"What was it?" Lexi asked. "My viewers would love to know!"

"Half a tonne of nonya," said Nani.

"Nonya?" Lexi tilted her head to one side. Ollie clamped his hand over his mouth as he realised what was coming.

"Nonya business!" Nani grinned, clearly delighted to have the chance to use my cousin Kish's favourite joke.

Lexi sighed with frustration as she turned off her phone and hurried after us. She grabbed my shoulder as I was about to climb into the back seat of Mrs Rutter's tiny vintage Mini.

"Look, Rani." She took a deep breath. "I'm sorry." I stared at her in amazement as she began gabbling at double speed without pausing for breath. "I was unprofessional and gave out your personal information in my video which I now realise was wrong. I promise it won't happen again and hope that you will accept my sincere apology."

It felt like she was rushing her way through something she had been told to say. My suspicions were confirmed when she turned to Ollie who was filming her on his own phone. "OK, see? I apologised."

"Got it," said Ollie, tapping the screen. "A once in a lifetime event! I'll send it straight to Mum."

Lexi gave me a stiff nod then stalked off to find more people to interview.

"I'm sorry too," said Ollie as I stood by the car while Mrs Rutter searched for her keys. "I told her not to put it up, but I should have said something to Mum when she did it anyway. She just doesn't think when she's chasing stories."

"It's not your fault," I said. "Anyway, how did you know we were here?"

"We went to your house this morning, but there was no one home. Mum had mentioned you were at Signal Rock yesterday. Your neighbour told us she hadn't seen you since then, so Lexi suggested we head here to ask if anyone had seen you return from the lighthouse."

"In case she could get a Steel Reveals out of it?" I said.

Ollie reddened. "Well, yeah, but she was actually the one who saw your sign on the video she was recording. She found out the name and owner of the boat you'd taken there and had the marina manager call Harrington Hall to—"

He was cut off by a growl from the engine and a loud bang as the car backfired.

"We really must be off!" called Mrs Rutter from the front seat.

"Chalo, Coco!" Nani ushered me into the car.

I waved goodbye to Ollie as Mrs Rutter pulled out of the parking space. I had to admit that I was impressed with Lexi. Although her approach was a bit reckless at times, she was pretty good at investigation. I was a bit confused by their story, though. Had the marina manager called Mrs Rutter as Ollie had told me, or had Mrs Rutter called them? It wouldn't surprise me if Lexi was trying to take credit for the rescue.

"Should we go home first and feed Cookie?" I asked Nani.

"He'll have plenty of food left," said Nani. "But if you're worried I'm sure Agnes won't mind taking us."

"Happy to," said the housekeeper. "Though you said you're going to Grennards. The bank closes early on a Friday."

The instructions were clear that the last part of the puzzle should be brought to the gallery while the exhibition was still on and today was the last day.

"Then we have to go straight there," I said.

"Excellent!" Mrs Rutter slammed her foot on the accelerator and we screeched out of the car park.

I clung on to the side handle as we whizzed through town, zipping through lights seconds before they turned red. It was kind of her to speed us to Grennards, but I'd really rather go slower and arrive in one piece.

I bounced forward against my seat belt as the car jerked to a halt at the bottom of the bank's steps.

"Thanks so much," said Nani as we jumped out. "I'll call to let you know how we get on."

"Call?" exclaimed Mrs Rutter. "Like you did last night? No, I'm waiting right here. Now go find that last piece of the puzzle. I can't wait to find out about the old rascal's secret and this mysterious reward!"

Nani squeezed my hand as we hurried up the steps. I patted the two stone lions out of habit before we went through the revolving wooden doors.

"Ayo!" said Nani as we entered a huge room with a mosaic-tiled floor, pillars of polished marble and a high ceiling festooned with chandeliers. At the far end was a row of old-fashioned wooden counters. Behind them sat well-groomed people in suits. It was the kind of bank you see in old movies – the sort of bank other banks wanted to be when they grew up. Was this where Lord Harrington had kept the millions everyone was obsessed with?

I felt weird standing in the fancy hall wearing yesterday's crumpled, paint-spattered clothes. I could tell Nani did too – she had taken off her coat and scarf and was smoothing down her tunic.

"May I help you?" asked a broad-shouldered man in a long jacket and top hat. I had *never* seen anyone wear a top hat in real life before and couldn't stop staring.

"Why hye believe you maaay," said Nani trying out a posh English accent. "One wishes to see Orion."

His eyes twinkled. "Do you have an appointment?" he asked.

"We have a letter for him," I blurted out as I realised I had been staring far too long. "From Lord Harrington."

The man smiled. "May I take your names?"

"Rani Devi Ramgoolam," I said, giving a little curtsy for some reason, then blushing.

"Sita Devi Ballah," said Nani, copying my curtsy.

He bowed back to us then gestured to a green leather sofa next to a gigantic vase of lilies. "Make yourselves comfortable. I shall speak to...ahem Orion forthwith."

"What does forthwith mean?" whispered Nani as we sat down as elegantly as we could despite the rude noises the leather sofa made under us.

"Straight away," I whispered back.

"Oh! I suppose this place can afford fancy words."

We put on our most serious faces and tried not to giggle as we waited and watched smartly dressed people coming and going. I wondered how rich you had to be to bank here.

The man with the top hat reappeared from a side room. "Please, come this way."

He held the door open for us as we entered

an office with a carpet so thick my feet sank into it like quicksand. A man in a waistcoat smiled as he got up from behind a huge desk and came over to shake hands with us.

"Ms Ballah, Ms Ramgoolam, pleased to meet you. I am Orion Aldridge, manager of Grennards bank. Do take a seat."

I'm not sure why, but I had expected the bank manager to be white, fat, loud and snooty, but Mr Aldridge was Black, slim and softly spoken. He looked about the same age as Nani. His grey moustache and goatee beard were extremely neat. I wondered if he combed and waxed them every day.

"Charles said that you had something for me?" He peered at us thoughtfully with his dark brown eyes as we settled into our seats.

I took out the envelope we had found in the lighthouse and slid it across the desk. Orion picked up a sword-shaped letter opener and slit open the envelope. After silently reading the letter inside, he slid it into his desk drawer and clapped his hands together.

"Congratulations are in order. You've cracked old Harry's puzzles!"

"Was he a friend of yours, Mr Aldridge?" I asked, surprised to hear him refer to Lord Harrington as "old Harry".

"A very good friend," said the bank manager. "And please, call me Orion. Harry would have been delighted to know that his clues were solved by two young ladies."

I rolled my eyes and looked at Nani, but she was fluttering her eyelashes and smoothing down her hair. I promised myself that no matter how old I got, I'd never be flattered by cheesy compliments.

"The other two items – do you have them with you?" he asked.

I nodded and patted my pocket containing the key card and the glass eye. "Do you know what we are supposed to do with them?"

"That's the last puzzle for you to solve." He smiled. "Follow me."

He led us back into the main hall, past the counters, to a door which he unlocked by placing his hand on a fingerprint reader.

"Ayo!" said Nani. "So high-tech!"

"Just because the bank is old, doesn't mean she's behind the times," said Orion as the door opened into a plain room with a gigantic, round steel door set into one wall. There were two small dials on the door, and a large metal wheel in the centre. The vault!

I stared at him. "We have to find a way to open that?"

"That's my job," said Orion. "Your puzzle lies within."

He stood with his back to us twiddling the dials, then turned the wheel in the centre. He stepped back as the huge door opened with a *clank*.

"Whoa!" I cried. It was at least a metre thick with dozens of sturdy metal bolts around the edges.

"You want us to go in there?" said Nani as Orion waved us through.

"That's where you'll find what you're looking for," he said.

I stepped into the vault, which was bigger than my bedroom. All that was in the room was a table and chairs. An odd-looking machine, like an old-fashioned computer, was set into the far wall.

"There's nothing in here," I said, puzzled.

"Oh, but there is," said Orion. "Millions of pounds' worth of valuables, and you have everything you need to access what you are looking for." He took out a stopwatch. "Harry was clear that you have no longer than fifteen minutes to use the objects you have found to obtain the final item. Good luck!"

"Wait! You're not going to lock us in, are you?" I called as he began closing the huge door.

"Don't worry, I'll open it in exactly fifteen minutes. If you want to leave sooner, just use the intercom and I'll let you straight out." He patted a little panel in the wall next to the door. "But that would be the end of your quest. Now, are you ready?"

I nodded, trying not to think about the metres of metal and concrete that would be between us and freedom. He clicked a timer on the top of his watch and closed the huge metal door behind him.

The bolts clunked into place and I felt the silence wrap around us. "OK, Nani," I said, pulling out the glass eye and the key card. "Let's get to work!"

CHAPTER TWELVE

The Vexing Vault

Nani and I went straight over to study the odd machine set into the wall. It had a round camera lens at the top. To the right was a narrow slot about six centimetres wide and beneath that was a screen. Nani was especially interested in the large metal drawer at the bottom. But it wouldn't open, no matter how much she pushed and pulled at it.

"No bashing!" I whispered sternly just in case Orion was watching us.

"As if I would suggest such a thing!" Nani grinned.

Three words flashed up on the screen:

INSERT IDENTITY CARD.

"It must mean this!" I held up the gold key card.

"Try it," said Nani.

I pushed the card into the slot. The screen flashed again:

PROCESSING...
PROCESSING...

I gripped Nani's hand as the machine gave an electronic *chirp*.

WELCOME, LORD HARRINGTON.
PLEASE LOOK DIRECTLY INTO THE LENS.
OPEN YOUR EYES WIDE AND TRY NOT TO BLINK.

"So *that*'s why he made this!" I held out my palm, revealing the copy of Lord Harrington's eye. "We need to scan it."

I pinched the glass eye between my fingers and held it up to the lens. The light above the lens flashed green then red. Another message flashed up on screen:

```
SCAN FAILED. TRY AGAIN.
TWO ATTEMPTS REMAINING.
```

"Sorry, Nani. I think my fingers were in the way."

I adjusted my grip. It was almost impossible to hold the glass eye with my fingertips without it slipping and by now my hands were shaking. As I lifted the eye up to the lens, the light began to flash again. Green, green...

I was clutching the eye so tightly that it popped right out of my fingers. Nani dived and caught it a split second before it hit the concrete floor.

"Good save, Nani!" I heaved a sigh of relief, then looked at the screen.

```
SCAN FAILED. TRY AGAIN.
ONE ATTEMPT REMAINING.
```

Only one chance left. If I didn't scan the eye properly this time, we'd never get our hands on whatever was in the vault. I couldn't trust my shaking hands.

"You do it," I told Nani.

"Oh no, Coco! My palms are too sweaty with all this pressure."

How on earth could we scan the eye? I thought for a moment then remembered something. "Nani, that gum you gave me at the lighthouse... Do you have any more?"

"Still missing your toothbrush?" she said as she rummaged through her bag. She handed me a piece of gum.

I chewed it a couple of times. Then I took a stubby pencil out of my pocket, pressed the gum on to the back of the eye and carefully stuck it to the pencil.

"An eye on a stick!" Nani laughed. "Now I've seen everything!"

Holding the pencil, I raised the eye to the lens and held my breath. The green light flashed as I counted. *One... Two... Three*.

The computer chirped.

SCAN ACCEPTED.

Nani patted me on the back and I let out my breath in a gasp. The screen flashed once more:

RETRIEVING SAFETY DEPOSIT BOX...

A series of clunking metallic noises came from within the walls.

"This is it, Nani!" I said. "How long do we have left?"

Nani checked her watch. "Seven minutes. Plenty of time!"

There was a whirring followed by the sound of something sliding down a chute and clunking into the metal drawer at the bottom of the machine. The drawer popped open with a *click*.

PLEASE TAKE YOUR SECURITY BOX.

Inside the drawer was a rectangular metal box, about the size of a large shoebox. I lifted it out and carried it to the table. Nani stood behind me, bangles jangling as she patted my shoulders.

"Quickly! Open it!"

My stomach sank as I stared down at it. "I...I can't." There was a keypad on the box. Above it was printed: *Enter your four-digit code.*

"Code? Code!" Nani slapped her hand on the table. "This is too much!" She marched over to the intercom by the door. "I'll call Mr Aldridge and tell him to open the box for us!"

"I think we have to work it out ourselves," I told her. "There must be a clue somewhere."

I took out my notebook and checked through each of Lord Harrington's letters. There was nothing I could see that might be a code.

"Four minutes to go," said Nani. "Let's just guess. How many combinations can there be?"

"Over two hundred," I said as she jabbed at the keypad. "*If* the numbers don't need to be in the correct order. It's over five thousand if they do." Dad loved teaching me maths puzzles at home. He had taught me about combinations last year when he caught me trying to guess the four-digit pin code on his tablet. I had been amazed at the number of possible combinations.

"Oh!" Nani sunk into the chair beside me as I kept searching. Was it something to do with the number of lines in each of the clues we had found? Or maybe the numbers were written in invisible ink on one of the letters? Lord Harrington had left clues for every other puzzle – why not this one?"

"Two minutes left," said Nani, looking glumly at her watch. "Are you sure there are no numbers on any of those letters. Or what about the key card?"

I shook my head. I was so mad at Lord Harrington. Why let us follow his whole silly trail then not give us the combination to the security box? Not even a clue.

"*The Clue!*" I shouted so loudly that Nani nearly fell off her chair. We *had* seen a four-digit number! I turned to the first page of my notebook and unfolded the copy I had made of Lord Harrington's painting. The number that gave the co-ordinates of the secret panel in his study. Could he have used it again?

My fingers shook as I typed it in. But my excitement died away as I pressed the last number and the box remained locked.

"That's it," I said. "I can't think of anything else it could be."

"Ninety seconds left," said Nani, looking over my shoulder. "Are there any other numbers in the picture? Or was there anything at the lighthouse?"

I shook my head. Then I remembered something. There *was* a number at the lighthouse! The numbers had also appeared on the clock with four hands in the painting. I quickly scanned through the pictures I had taken. There it was, the date above the lighthouse door.

"1847!" I yelled. "It's 1847."

"Thirty seconds left," said Nani. "Quick, try it!"

My fingers trembled as I jabbed the numbers on the keypad – *one, eight, four…* I stopped, smiled at Nani and pushed the box towards her.

"You do the last one."

"We'll do it together!" She hugged me tight to her side and together we pressed the seven. The lid popped open.

We whooped in triumph and were still dancing around the room when the vault door opened.

"You did it!" said Orion as he stepped inside. "Congratulations!"

"Mersi!" Nani grabbed him by the shoulders and kissed him on both cheeks.

"Er, quite…" He adjusted his glasses awkwardly.

"What's inside?" asked Nani as I reached into the box. "Show us!"

I frowned as I lifted out the contents – a metal-bound, padlocked book.

"I think it's a diary."

"That's right," said Orion. "Harry's diary."

"The dire confession." I rolled my eyes. "Dire-ee confession. It's here in this diary?"

197

"Exactly," said the bank manager. "How like Harry to almost make a pun of it. The letter states that you must take this diary to Ms Boyd at the gallery. She has the key and will present the prize after reading out Harry's secret. I must say, as much as I dislike scandal, I'm intrigued to hear what it is!"

Orion checked his watch. "The gallery is open for another hour and a half. That leaves more than enough time to get there. I have to help close up here so I'll join you later. But I'll call the gallery and let Ms Boyd know to expect the victor soon. I'm sure she'll want to gather an audience and arrange for the press to be there too."

I clutched the diary to my chest. I was as interested to learn Lord Harrington's secret as I was to find out about our prize. Could the secret be something to do with his missing fortune?

"What are you waiting for?" Orion shooed us out of the vault and back through the bank.

We waved goodbye and hurried down the steps to where Mrs Rutter was waiting in her car. She rolled down her window and her eyes lit up when she saw what I was holding.

"The last piece of the puzzle! I knew you could do it!" She beamed. "Can I see it?"

I handed her the diary. She turned it over, looking for a way to open it.

"It's locked," said Nani. "We need to take it to Ms Boyd at the art gallery. She has the key and the prize. Thank you so much for waiting for us."

"Just a moment," said the housekeeper as Nani reached for the passenger door. "I have something to show you too." She handed me a white square of card the size of a drink coaster.

As I took it, I noticed that as well as her bandaged arms, her hands were covered in scratches. I turned the card over. It was a photo from a polaroid camera. I gasped when I realised what I was looking at – a picture of Cookie. He was in a tiny cage, flapping and squawking at the person taking the photo.

"What is this?" Nani looked from the photo to Mrs Rutter then lunged through the window for the diary. Mrs Rutter pulled it from her grasp, threw it into the back seat and wound up the window.

I tried the rear door. It was locked.

"What's going on?" I shouted, hammering on the glass.

"An exchange," called the housekeeper, winding down the window a crack. "The bird for the diary. I'll take this to the gallery and retrieve my millions, then I'll send you a message telling you where to find your bird. Try to stop me collecting what I'm owed and your vicious little vulture will starve in that cage."

I stared, unable to believe my ears. Sweet old Mrs Rutter was stealing our prize from under us. And if we wanted to see Cookie again, we had to let her do it! She had clearly fallen for the rumour that the prize was a fortune!

"You went to our house while we were trapped on Signal Rock, didn't you?" I cried. *No wonder she wanted us to go straight to the bank instead of heading home first.*

"Why do you think the fuel tank was half empty?" She smirked. "Couldn't risk you getting in Billy's way when he went to your house last night, like your wretched bird did the night he went to look for the key card and eye!" She dropped a set of keys over the top of the window.

"My keys!" shouted Nani snatching them up. "You pickpocket! You sly thief! Birdnapper!"

"So Billy *is* in on this too?" I said, kicking myself for starting to think I'd misjudged him.

"Oh, this was all his idea. And if you get in our way, one call to him will make sure you never see Cookie again."

"How could you?" I shouted. "Imagine if someone did that to Lucky and Peaches!"

"I haven't seen Lucky and Peaches in thirty years!" Mrs Rutter laughed. "They were my husband's birds. How could anyone like budgies? Horrible, screechy things. He thought it was an accident when they got out and flew away. Good job I kept their cage, though. It certainly came in handy!"

"You're awful," I told her. "Why didn't you just try to solve the puzzles yourself?"

"You seemed to be enjoying the hunt." She grinned triumphantly. "And I've already put up with decades of Hare-brained Harrington's nonsense. I was going to head to Signal Rock today to offer your bird's return in exchange for everything you'd found so far, but then that awful video girl drew everyone's attention to the fact you were trapped."

"You mean Lexi," I put in.

"Anyway, she was going to call the coastguard so we had to hurry out to rescue you and play it nice for the cameras. When you said there was something else left to solve, I thought – why not let you do the rest of the work too?"

"Why, you rotten—" Nani shouted. She grabbed the top of the car window and tried to force it down.

"Help! Save me!" screeched Mrs Rutter. Nani froze for a second. Everyone in the street was staring.

"If you even think of calling the police," she hissed, "Billy will make sure you never see your bird again. As I said, you'll get the rotten creature back once I collect my millions!" At that, she stomped on the accelerator and screeched off down the street, leaving a cloud of smoke behind her.

I stared after the car, fists clenched and shaking. "What do we do now?"

Nani shook her head. "I don't know, Coco. I don't know."

CHAPTER THIRTEEN

Cookie Chaos

I stared at the photo of Cookie. He looked so upset, beak open mid-screech, but at least he didn't appear hurt. Where was he? How could we save him? My fists were clenched so tightly my fingernails dug into my palms.

"Let me see that photo," said Nani, sitting down on the steps. I sat beside her and handed it over. I couldn't bear looking at it any more.

"Look at this," she said at last.

"I don't want to," I told her, turning away as she tried to hand it back. Nani shook my shoulder until I finally took the photo.

"See the garden tools next to the cage?" she said. "It looks as though he's in some sort of shed. Now see this..." She pointed at something behind the cage.

The photo was dark, I had to strain my eyes to make out the shape. Was that...a steering wheel? There was something painted on the arch above it – a red and yellow pattern. Flames.

I gripped Nani's arm. "That's Lord Harrington's golf cart! The one you drove to the maze. So Cookie must be..."

"In Billy's work shed at Harrington Hall!" said Nani.

"We have to save him!" I cried. Mrs Rutter could have the prize – all I wanted now was Cookie, safe and sound.

"Mrs Ballah!" a man's voice called out. "I'm glad you're still here." Orion was hurrying down the steps with Nani's scarf in his hand. "You left this in my office."

"Is everything all right?" he asked as Nani took it. "I thought you'd be straight off to the gallery."

He pinched his goatee and listened, wide-eyed, as Nani told him what had happened.

Orion shook his head and let out a long sigh. "I knew Harry didn't really trust Mrs Rutter, but he would never have guessed she was capable of something like this. And I'm surprised about Billy. He's fiercely protective of Harrington Hall's grounds, but I never thought of him as cruel or dishonest."

"We know where Cookie is, but Mrs Rutter said Billy is guarding him," I said. "If we go to the police Billy might hurt him."

"In the meantime, that terrible woman is going to claim Rani's reward!" Nani put in.

"That won't do at all," said Orion. "Wait here." He hurried back into the bank, returning with the tall man in the top hat. "Charles is the best security guard we have ever had. He was in the army for twenty-five years before coming to join us."

"At your service." Charles gave us a sharp salute.

"He'll make sure you get your parrot back.

Charles, you may take Lizzie."

Charles's eyes widened in surprise. He gave a little nod then hurried off round the corner. I wondered who Lizzie was – another security guard?

"My number." Orion gave Nani his business card. "I'll go straight to the gallery to delay things and keep Mrs Rutter there. I won't let anyone know what is happening until you call to tell me Cookie is safe."

"Thanks so much," I said.

"Keep me updated," he called. He looked quite excited by all the drama as he rushed off to his own car.

"With him on our side, maybe we'll be able to rescue Cookie *and* get to the gallery in time to stop that woman," said Nani as she texted Orion her number.

I didn't reply. The only thing on my mind was finding Cookie and never letting him out of my sight again.

"Ayo!" exclaimed Nani as a beautiful old silver sports car pulled around the corner.

Charles leaned out of the window and waved at us to jump in. There was something familiar looking about the car. As I slid along the leather seat in the back it dawned on me. "This is like James Bond's car!" Dad makes me watch all those old movies with him. He always says if he wasn't a maths tutor, he'd be a secret agent.

"Well spotted, Agent Ramgoolam," said Charles with a smile. "Lizzie here is a vintage Aston Martin. She's Mr Aldridge's pride and joy. This is our first real mission, so we'd better not get into any dangerous car chases. Buckle up. Lizzie and I will get you to Harrington Hall in no time."

"I'm a very good driver," said Nani. "Maybe I could..."

"I don't think your licence is valid here!" I said quickly, with no idea whether that was actually true. Seeing Nani behind the wheel of a golf cart, there was no way I wanted to be in the back as she drove a super spy's car!

Lizzie's engine roared as Charles zipped out of the town centre. The car was even older than Nani and had a lovely leathery smell. The countryside whizzed past as we followed the winding country roads that led to Harrington Hall. Despite my seat belt, I kept sliding into Nani as we zoomed around each bend. I had always thought Dad drove too slowly, but after riding with Nani, Mrs Rutter and now Charles, I just wanted a driver who didn't make me want to close my eyes the whole way. At least every speedy bend brought me that bit closer to Cookie.

When we finally arrived at the hall, Charles clicked a little button and the gates opened slowly in front of us.

"You've got a key?" I asked in surprise.

"Of course," said Charles. "Mr Aldridge and Lord Harrington were very good friends. In fact, Lizzie was a gift from Lord Harrington." He parked behind a tall hedge. "We'll leave the old girl here so Billy doesn't see us coming."

We got out of the car and crept up the drive, staying under cover of the trees and bushes.

I kept an eye out for Billy as we slipped round the side of the building and headed for the gardens.

Nani's phone buzzed. "It's Orion," she whispered, showing me the message.

Rutter already handed over diary. Harry's secret to be read and prize awarded at 5pm. Will try to delay but get your skates on.

I looked at my watch – we had only thirty minutes to find Cookie and get to the museum.

"This is it," I told Charles, pointing to Billy's work shed. "We think Cookie's in there."

Charles motioned for us to stay where we were as he slipped through the bushes towards the shed. I peeped through the foliage. *Please be careful*, I thought as I watched him reach the shed and try the doors. Was Billy in there, waiting for us? He probably wouldn't expect anyone to realise where he was keeping Cookie.

Charles seemed satisfied that no one was on lookout and beckoned us over. He lifted me up to peer in through one of the windows. The cage was on the floor, exactly where we'd seen it in the photo, right next to the golf cart.

The second Cookie saw me he grasped the bars with his claws, flapping his wings.

POOR COOKIE! CALL THE COPS! WAOW-WAOW-WAOW-WAOW-WAOW!

"Hey, Cookie!" I called, tapping the window lightly with my fingertips until he stopped his siren. I couldn't bear to hear him so upset. "We're here now. We'll get you out soon." He screeched even louder at the sound of my voice.

WAOW-WAOW-WAOW-WAOW-WAOW!

"The doors are locked *and* chained shut," said Charles as he put me down. "And Billy had security glass put in after some expensive tools were stolen last year. I'll need a hammer to break it."

"Please don't try!" I said. "The glass could hit Cookie."

"Is there another way?" asked Nani.

Charles tested the doors with his shoulder then scratched his cheek. "Wait here a minute," he said. "I'll check what tools are in the car."

I stood on an overturned bucket to look through the window again. Cookie was gnawing the bars of the cage.

POOR COOKIE. GO TO PRISON, COOKIE. WAOW-WAOW-WAOW-WAOW-WAOW!

"We're coming. We'll let you out soon!" I shouted. I wanted to cram Mrs Rutter into that tiny cage.

Charles seemed to be taking forever. If only there was something I could do. *Wait, maybe I could!* I pulled out my notebook and slid off two of the paper clips I'd used to attach cuttings in there.

"This is no time for working on your story," said Nani in amazement.

"I'm not," I said as I straightened out the metal clips. "I'm getting Cookie out!" Last Christmas I had taught myself to pick locks in the hope of finding my presents. I hadn't found any, but I *had* learned how to open a few different types of locks and this padlock looked fairly easy.

"Here goes," I whispered to myself. I slid one paper clip into the bottom of the lock then pushed the other into the top and wriggled it through the lock's tumblers. I pulled the bottom paper clip to the side as I heard the clicks I was listening for.

Nani held her breath as she watched me work. She clapped her hands as the padlock sprang open and I pulled the chains from the handle.

"One more to go," I said, inspecting the lock on the work-shed door. *This one could be tricky.*

"GET AWAY FROM MY WORK SHED!"

The shout from behind us sent an icy chill down my spine. I spun round to see Billy storming towards us. Nani pushed me behind her as I looked around wildly for Charles.

"NO! *You* get away from *us*!" Nani shouted in an even louder voice. Billy paused and stared at Nani. Her fists were raised and she looked ready for a fight.

"I'll call the police," he said. "You're not stealing my cart and tearing up the gardens again."

"What?" I said. How could he think we wanted to joyride in his golf cart when he had Cookie held captive in his shed?

"Call them," said Nani. "Go on! You're the one who should be in prison!"

GO TO PRISON! POOR COOKIE! Cookie squawked mournfully from the shed.

Billy stared at the door, eyes wide.

"Back away, Billy!" cried Charles, bursting through the bushes with a huge spanner in one hand, a snow shovel in the other. Billy backed up so fast he tripped and fell in a heap.

"Charles?" He held up his hands as the security guard loomed over him. "What's going on?"

"What's going on?" repeated Charles, pointing the spanner towards the shed. "Well, first we're going to rescue the parrot, then I'm calling the police. And then we're off to the gallery to stop your accomplice from stealing Rani's prize."

Billy stared at us all as if the whole world had gone mad.

"What parrot?" he finally spat out. With perfect timing, Cookie let out a loud, bullfrog croak followed by a cackle of laughter.

"There's a parrot in there! But...how?" Billy really was a brilliant actor.

"Just open the door, Billy," ordered Charles.

The groundskeeper got up and fumbled for his keys. "Who did this?"

"You're trying to convince us you're not working hand in hand with Agnes Rutter?" asked Nani.

"That ratbag!" growled Billy. "Is that why she's had me running errands all day? So I wouldn't be around to notice she'd been in my shed."

As Billy went through his keys, I noticed his hands and wrists. I thought about Mrs Rutter's bandages. There was no way Cookie would let anyone take him without a fight and Billy's skin was completely free of peck marks and scratches. *Hadn't Charles said he always thought Billy was trustworthy?*

"He's not acting," I said to Nani as Billy unlocked the door. "Mrs Rutter took Cookie from the house and got a good pecking. That's why her arms were bandaged. I don't think Billy was involved at all."

"So she was just been trying to make us think she had back up?" said Nani. "Wait till I see her!"

The moment Billy threw open the doors, I dashed inside and unfastened the cage.

I ducked as Cookie shot out into the fresh air, revelling in his freedom.

He circled the shed a couple of times then flew down to my shoulder and snuggled against my cheek, making little chirps and whistles and muttering, GOOD COOKIE, PRETTY COOKIE.

I saw some water and little pieces of fruit in the cage. At least Mrs Rutter wasn't a complete monster.

"Sorry we left you all alone," I whispered, rubbing my face in his feathers.

Billy stared at us. "I had nothing to do with this," he said. "You've got to believe me."

"I do," I said, kissing Cookie's beak.

"Mrs Rutter packed up all her things this morning," he said. "She can't be planning on coming back. I'll wait around just in case, but you should get down to the gallery to stop her."

"I don't think we *can*." I glanced at my watch. "Fifteen minutes until the prize is awarded, then she's gone."

"Cookie is safe now," said Charles. "Mr Aldridge will be doing everything he can to stall the prize-giving. If we're quick, you can stop her and tell everyone what happened."

"Oh, we'll stop her!" Nani's bangles jangled as she shook the shoulders of an imaginary Mrs Rutter.

I wasn't bothered about Lord Harrington's secret or the mysterious prize any longer. Nothing mattered now that I had Cookie back. But then there was the fact that Mrs Rutter had broken into our home, trapped us at sea, taken *my* bird hostage, framed Billy – *and* she wanted rewarding for it...

"Chalo?" asked Nani.

I rolled up my sleeves. "Chalo!" I growled.

CHAPTER FOURTEEN

Disguises and Prizes

I held the cage tight on my lap as Charles sped us back into town. Cookie wasn't happy about being locked up again, but we couldn't risk him flapping around the inside of the car as Lizzie whizzed down country lanes, practically sliding around the corners.

Nani was in the front passenger seat trying to call Orion. "I can't get through!" She shook the phone as if that would help.

"Let me try," said Charles. "Call **MISTER ALDRIDGE,**" he said loudly to the phone mounted on the dashboard. The phone lit up then beeped. **Call failed** appeared on the screen. "His battery must have run out. Don't worry. He'll stall until we get there."

"I hope so," said Nani. "Please hurry."

We pulled up in front of the gallery at five o'clock exactly. There were two TV vans outside. Word must have spread that the diary had been found and Lord Harrington's secrets were about to be revealed. No doubt Lexi was already there streaming one of her Steel Reveals. I paused for a moment, wondering what to do with Cookie.

"Leave him with me," said Charles. "He can sit on the steering wheel and we'll have a little chat until you're done."

"Behave and mind your language," I told Cookie as we jumped out of the car.

MiND YOUR LANGUAGE! PULL UP YOUR SOCKS! BLOW YOUR NOSE! ACHOO!

I thanked Charles, then grabbed Nani's hand and raced up the steps to the gallery. As I sprinted past the man on the front desk, who didn't even look up from his paper, Orion's voice boomed out through the whole gallery's speaker system.

"...and after his success at sea, Lord Harrington took on his greatest challenge yet – the art world!"

"*Please*, Mr Aldridge," came a voice I recognised as belonging to Ms Boyd. "Lord Harrington's life story is a swashbuckling tale of adventure, but we simply must move things along."

"And as you can see by the work around you, he was quite the artist," Orion continued.

"He's still stalling," I told Nani. "It's not too late!"

We rounded the corner into the corridor that led to the main gallery. "Oh no!" I cried as I saw it was packed with people. The doors to the gallery were closed and a tall security guard was standing in front of them arguing with someone. *Lexi!*

"You have to let us in!" Lexi insisted as Ollie hung back behind her. "We have hundreds of viewers on our channel. They're all waiting to hear Lord Harrington's big reveal!"

The guard raised her eyebrow. "The gallery is at capacity. Press and special guests only."

I cringed as Lexi actually used the words not even the world's most famous pop stars should ever say... "Don't you know who I am?"

"There's no way we're getting past her," I said to Nani, nodding towards the security guard, who was still blocking Lexi's way.

With his phone dead we couldn't even call Orion to let him know we were there. I flopped against the wall. We were so close. Was there nothing we could do to stop Mrs Rutter accepting our prize?

"Move aside, coming through." The crowd parted briefly to let a woman in overalls out of the door that led to the café. She was pushing a cart containing a large bin and a mop and bucket.

"I've got an idea," said Nani. "Follow me."

I stayed close to Nani as she padded after the cart then ducked behind a pillar to watch as the cleaner disappeared into a side room near the gallery entrance. She came out a minute later without the cart and overalls, waving cheerily to the man at the admission desk as she left the building.

"Night, Stu. Don't let that lot mess up my floors."

"Night, Gloria," Stu called back, without looking up from his paper.

"Why are we hiding behind a pillar spying on the cleaner?" I whispered.

"Because this is how we're going to get past that guard!" said Nani. "Chalo, Coco!"

I followed her to the door the cleaner had just come from. I was glad that the man on the front desk was too engrossed in his paper to see Nani's sneaky tiptoe walk, which made it completely obvious that we were up to something.

"Quick!" Nani hissed as she opened the door and pulled me into a room full of mops, brooms and buckets.

"What now?" I asked, but I was starting to get the picture as she grabbed a set of overalls from a hook on the back of the door and put them on, rolling up the legs and sleeves to fit.

"There aren't any in my size," I said, looking around.

"I'm afraid no one will believe the gallery has a ten-year-old cleaner," said Nani.

"Then what am I supposed to… Oh!" Nani had opened the lid of the bin and was giving me an impish smile. I sighed as I realised her plan.

Gloria had emptied it and put in a clean bin bag, but there was still a lingering pong. *This is no time to worry about getting a bit smelly!* I told myself as I stepped up on to a stool, took a deep breath and lowered myself into the bin. It was embarrassing, but maybe not half as embarrassing as asking someone *Don't you know who I am?*

"Oh, Rani!" Nani laughed. "Painting on bed-sheets, picking locks, hiding in bins! What would your mum and dad say?"

"I won't tell if you don't. Now can you get us to the main gallery?"

Nani bundled her hair into a hair-net. "No problem! Now, lid on."

I could hear Nani thoroughly enjoying her role as the cart trundled out of the cupboard and through the reception area.

"Evening, Stu," she called. "Gloria said she'd emptied the bins, but just shout if you want me to polish your desk for you."

I lifted the bin lid slightly and saw the man on the desk give Nani a nod over the top of his paper. I was impressed at Nani for remembering their names and using them to sound as though she worked there too. I almost believed her myself. She was very good at undercover work. It was amazing how invisible she could be while actually being extremely visible.

"Make way!" Nani called to the crowd in the corridor. "Emergency cleaner coming through!"

The crowd had no choice as Nani barged through with the cart, using a soggy mop to nudge anyone who didn't move. In no time at all we were at the large doors that led to the main gallery. Even Lexi stopped arguing with the guard to jump out of the way of Nani's mop.

I could hear Orion still playing for time.

Ms Boyd's voice crackled through the speakers, interrupting Orion's story. "Darling, thank you for your delightful memories, but now the show must go on."

"Press and special guests only," the guard said firmly to Nani.

"Of course, Charity," said Nani, reading the guard's name tag which I could just see through the tiny gap where I'd pushed up the bin lid. "But we're not guests, we're working."

"We?" said the guard. I gritted my teeth at Nani's slip of the tongue.

"Me and…my mop!" Nani said, recovering brilliantly. "Someone was sick over the mayor's shoes. If you can't let us in then maybe you could save me a job and mop it up yourself?"

The offer was enough to make up the guard's mind. She opened the doors and ushered Nani through.

"Hey!" cried Lexi, who had clearly just been caught trying to follow us in.

Peering out from under the lid, I could see that the gallery was full of photographers and important people all waiting to hear Lord Harrington's secrets. There was Mayor Slater, our local MP. Lady Hardright – the richest woman in Camberford. Jonny Ronson – the manager of Camberford Rovers, and his much younger, golden-haired wife. The journalists and presenters from the local radio station and TV channel hovered close to the stage where Ms Boyd was standing beside Lord Harrington's portrait.

I frowned as I spotted Camera Guy, his hair still tied up in that little bun as he snapped away. Who *was* he?

Ms Boyd had finally wrestled the microphone from Orion. Mrs Rutter stood beside her, looking smug.

"Ooh, I'll mop that smile off her face," muttered Nani, waving her mop as she pushed our way to the middle of the crowd. The cart bumped up and down to the occasional yelp as she ran over a few stubborn feet.

"Darlings! Thank you so very much for coming at such short notice," said Ms Boyd. "I am thrilled to announce that Agnes Rutter, Harrington Hall's housekeeper, has solved all of the clues and located the final puzzle piece – Lord Harrington's diary."

The crowd applauded as Ms Boyd held up the diary. Cameras clicked, reporters scribbled.

"And now it's time to reveal Lord Harrington's mysterious prize!"

"The missing millions!" gasped several members of the crowd.

Mrs Rutter held out her hands as Ms Boyd brought out a golden envelope. I couldn't bear it a second longer.

"**STOP!**" I shouted at the top of my voice as I threw back the bin lid with a bang.

Hundreds of eyes stared at me as I stood in the bin, fist raised like a gladiator in a stinky chariot.

"She didn't find the diary!" I yelled, clambering out of the bin to stand on top of the cart. "We did. Me and my nani!"

The entire crowd was staring at us as Nani tore off her overalls, yanked off her hair-net and shook out her hair like an actress in one of her favourite cheesy soap operas.

I turned to glare directly at Mrs Rutter whose eyes had almost popped out of her head like a squeezy rubber chicken's. She grabbed the microphone.

"How dare you! Of course I found the diary. I was Lord Harrington's housekeeper for forty-five years. I know how he thinks better than anyone. Now let's hurry this along. Hey, get off!" she shouted as Orion wrestled the mic from her and shouted into it:

"She's lying!"

Ms Boyd stood open-mouthed as chaos unfolded around her.

"Stop that!" yelped Mrs Rutter as a wet sponge bounced off her head. Nani was barging her way to the stage, shaking her mop and brandishing another sponge.

Orion finally grabbed the microphone and beckoned us towards him. Mrs Rutter tried to pull it back from him, then froze. A police siren was wailing in the distance.

WAOW-WAOW-WAOW-WAOW-WAOW!

It grew louder and louder. Too loud.

WAOW-WAOW-WAOW-WAOW-WAOW!

"Is... Is there a police car *inside* the building?" stammered Ms Boyd, dazedly. Just at that moment, Mrs Rutter lunged forward and snatched the golden envelope.

"Stop, thief!" yelled Nani, battling through the crowd with her mop as the housekeeper bolted for the door.

Mrs Rutter flung it open and charged straight into the security guard. The siren filled the room as Cookie whooshed over their heads and into the gallery.

WAOW-WAOW-WAOW-WAOW-WAOW!

Cookie stopped wailing and screeched with delight as he spotted me. He swooped over to land on my shoulder and wolf-whistled at the surprised crowd. Charles appeared in the doorway and shot us an apologetic shrug as I hopped down from the cart. I should have known he'd be no match for Cookie.

Mrs Rutter tried to duck between Charles and the security guard, but they were ready for her. Charles plucked the envelope from her hand as the guard took hold of her arm.

Ms Boyd finally recovered enough to speak. "Thank you, Charity. And er...?"

"Charles," said Charles, weaving his way through the crowd to hand her the envelope. Ms Boyd smoothed her hair and adjusted her huge black and white ballerina skirt.

"Charity, bring Mrs Rutter here." She nodded towards me and Nani. "You two had better come up on stage too."

I'LL TAKE IT FROM HERE!

Mrs Rutter held her hand in front of her face as photographers clicked away, while Nani merrily posed for them, holding her mop like a royal sceptre. Cookie bounced on my

233

shoulder, copying the sound of clicking cameras as I stroked his feathers to calm him.

"Now *who* found this diary?" asked Ms Boyd holding it up.

"I did!" shouted Mrs Rutter.

"Oooooh! You did not!" cried Nani, shaking the mop at her. "This cheat broke into our home, then trapped us in a lighthouse."

"And she birdnapped and ransomed my parrot," I added.

"Break-ins, lighthouses, stolen parrots, ransoms?" said Ms Boyd. "Someone, *please* explain what on earth has been going on!"

"It was my Rani who solved the clues and found the diary!" Nani beamed.

"I couldn't have done it without Nani," I added.

RANi! RANi! GOOD GiRL, RANi! shrieked Cookie. BLOW YOUR NOSE! PULL UP YOUR SOCKS!

"It's true," said Orion. "The diary was hidden in Lord Harrington's safety deposit box at my bank." He whipped out the letter we had given him. "These ladies brought me *this* letter from

Lord Harrington himself. Only the person who had solved the clues would have it."

The crowd oooohed as the bank manager opened the letter and read it aloud.

Dearest Orion,

The bearer of this letter has solved my riddles, faced the minotaur and visited Signal Rock with my old friend, the Dancing Deacon. Now the final challenge awaits.

On receipt of this letter, open the vault for them and set the clock to fifteen minutes. If they are as clever as I believe they must be, they will figure out how to access the deposit box containing my diary. Then my most dire confession can be revealed.

Yours,

Harry

Orion sniffed and gave a cough that might have covered a little sob. He handed the letter to Ms Boyd. She looked it over, then turned to Mrs Rutter with narrowed eyes.

"It was the groundskeeper, Billy!" the housekeeper cried. "He made me do it."

"Rubbish!" I cried. "He helped us rescue Cookie. He had nothing to do with your plan."

Mrs Rutter opened her mouth but nothing came out. She had finally run out of lies.

"You kidnapped this girl's bird and took the diary so that you could collect the prize for yourself," said Ms Boyd, looking over the top of her glasses as the crowd gasped.

"Oh, don't talk down to me, Ms Fancy Pants!" shouted Mrs Rutter. "I served that batty old fool for forty-five years and what did I get for it? Not one penny! Why *shouldn't* I get a bit of what I'm due?"

"That's not exactly true, is it?" said Orion quietly. "You got far more than a penny."

"You mean my wages?" She sniffed. "OK, he didn't pay badly, but I served that man well..."

"And that's why he didn't fire you, or report you to the police," said Orion.

Mrs Rutter stared at him. "Wha... I mean, how..." She trailed off.

"Yes. He knew about the money you took from his pockets," continued Orion. "The silver that went missing, the vases and artworks that mysteriously vanished and turned up at auctions."

Mrs Rutter's mouth opened and shut like a goldfish. Murmurs broke out all around us.

"Nothing left to say?" asked Nani.

YOU'RE GOING TO JAIL, PAL! shouted Cookie as if he understood exactly what was going on. Everyone laughed.

"Charity!" Ms Boyd called the security guard over and whispered something to her. Charity put her hand on Mrs Rutter's shoulder and led her from the room. I wondered if they were going to call the police. It was hard to feel sorry for Mrs Rutter after everything she had done.

"Apologies, my sweets," said Ms Boyd over the voices of the special guests, who were all gossiping about the revelations. At the back of the room I noticed Redbeard had joined the crowd, empty-handed and looking rather grumpy about it. Though after making a big donation to get into Harrington Hall, it didn't sound as though he had any need of a reward!

Ms Boyd cringed as she saw journalists making notes about the unfolding events. Their pencils were moving so quickly that smoke seemed to be coming from the ends.

"Of course, the real story here is whatever lies in this diary. Let's get on. Rani...?"

"Ramgoolam," prompted Orion.

"Rani Ramgoolam!" Ms Boyd held up the golden envelope. "On behalf of the late Lord Harrington, I award you this prize."

The photographers snapped away as she put her arm round my shoulder and handed me the envelope.

"What are you waiting for, Coco?" Nani grinned.

The crowd leaned forward as I tore it open. Inside was a sheaf of papers. At the top of the pile there was a letter, addressed: *To the finder of my diary.*

The papers were full of complicated sentences that I didn't understand. I passed them to Orion, unfolded the letter and read it out loud.

My dear seeker of secrets,

Your sharp mind and keen eye have led you well. Our journey together may be over, but to remember it I offer you the guardianship of my greatest luxury...

I paused as the crowd whispered among themselves, still convinced that the prize would be Lord Harrington's fortune.

...my home from home, my source of artistic inspiration, my window into the wonders of the universe — the lighthouse on Signal Rock. Share her with others as I am sharing her with you, and may life bring you joy, adventure and many more mysteries to solve.

"Guardianship? What does that mean?" I asked, looking from Ms Boyd to Orion.

"It means that old Harry is leaving the lighthouse in your care," said the bank manager, shuffling through the papers. "You can decide what to do with it. However, you cannot sell it and many, many years from now, you must pass it on to a new guardian. There's an allowance for its upkeep and he has also left you the *Dancing Deacon* to travel out there. There's lots more detail in here that we can run through later with your parents. I doubt Harry expected it to go to such a young victor, though I'm sure he would have been delighted!"

My legs wobbled and I sat down hard on the stage. So that's how the prize was of immense yet little value, as Ms Boyd had announced at the start. I wasn't being given the lighthouse, but I was getting to borrow it for a lifetime.

"Is this... Is this for real?" I asked Ms Boyd, who was reading the papers over Orion's shoulder.

"Absolutely, darling girl!" She beamed. "You are now the guardian of Signal Rock lighthouse *and* captain of your own boat."

"Oh, my Coco!" Nani swept me up into the biggest, squeeziest hug. "I'm so proud of you." My head spun as cameras flashed. Over the heads of the crowd I saw even Redbeard begrudgingly join in the applause.

"Rani! Hetty Phelps, from *The Chronicle*," chirped a woman with short, curly black hair and a little red hat adorned with cherries. She thrust a microphone into my face. "How do you feel about becoming guardian of one of our most famous landmarks?"

Another microphone appeared. "Mike Jones, *The Journal*," barked a broad-shouldered, grey-haired man, "What are you going to do with it? Live in it? Rent it out?"

"I don't know," I said, feeling as if the whole world had flipped upside down and inside out.

A camera light shone in my face as a third big fluffy microphone appeared above my head. "Rami, our viewers would love to know how you found the diary," called a man I vaguely recognised from the local evening news.

I blinked against the light.

"It's Rani, not Rami," was all I managed to say before Cookie landed on the microphone and squawked, **CLEVER RANI! PULL UP YOUR SOCKS!** He then cackled so loudly that the man holding the mic had to yank off his headphones.

"Rani!" shouted Lexi. I guessed she had seized the opportunity to duck into the gallery while Charity was busy. Ollie was holding his phone above the heads of the reporters to capture my face. "Lexi Steel from Steel Reveals. Don't-forget-to-like-and-subscribe. How do you feel about being the best investigator in Camberford?"

"Investigative journalist!" I grinned. "I'm going to be writing a news article all about Lord Harrington's puzzle path."

"We can't wait to read it!" Ollie called.

"Us too!" said another voice from the crowd. I blushed as I saw her name tag and realised it was the editor of the *Camberford Herald* – the very person who would be heading up the judging panel of the Junior Journalist competition.

"Fancy a job at *The Chronicle*?" called Hetty Phelps to cheers from the crowd.

"Move back, my dears." Ms Boyd waved everyone away. "Rani hasn't finished reading her letter."

I looked down at the half-crumpled letter in my hand and continued to read.

My last request is that you turn to the page bookmarked in my diary and read my secret shame for all to hear. Maybe your keen mind can solve one last mystery and find my hidden treasure.

Your friend,

Rupert Harrington

"The missing millions!" Lexi squealed. So there *was* a hidden treasure after all?

As whispers of anticipation rippled through the audience, Ms Boyd took a key out of her pocket and inserted it into the lock on the diary. The metal binding sprung open. She turned to a page bookmarked with a leather oak leaf and handed the diary back to me. At the top of the page was the heading: **My Dire Confession**. This was it – the terrible secret Lord Harrington had been teasing us all with. What could it be? And would it lead to his missing fortune?

CHAPTER FIFTEEN

A Dire Confession

Ms Boyd held out her microphone for me to read Lord Harrington's confession. Unsurprisingly, it was written in verse. I took a deep breath.

I'll try to keep this statement brief,
As I reveal – I am a thief!

The audience gasped as one. Journalists scribbled furiously.

Now you may think me quite a fool,
But my victims were all very cruel.

Lady Hardright, downright rude.
Was never happy with her food.
She'd send staff dashing from the hall
And hurled her meals against the wall.

"I say! Stop reading this instant!" shrieked Lady Hardright from the crowd, to a chorus of shushing from the rest of the room.

"Go on, chicken," urged Ms Boyd as Lady Hardright looked as though she was about to burst.

When I was visiting for tea,
She fired two maids in front of me.
When I asked the reason why,
She said she liked to watch them cry.
Bad deeds should not go unheeded,
Punishment was sorely needed.
It niggled at me for some time
And thus began my life of crime.
I cracked her safe and from her things,
I took some ruby earrings.
In the safe I left a letter,
Advising her to treat folk better.

Everyone turned to look for a response from Lady Hardright, but she had already made a swift exit.

My next theft came just two months later,
A golden watch from Mayor Slater.

The mayor smiled, took a couple of steps back, then shot off hot on the heels of Lady Hardright, without even waiting to hear what Lord Harrington had accused him of.

"I wish he'd answer our letters that fast!" called out an elderly woman to a chorus of laughter as I began to read the mayor's misdeed.

I'd seen him chase and kick a cat,
For lying on his new doormat...

I paused and scanned the rest of the page, then the next, and the next. "There's too much to read out!" I whispered to Ms Boyd. "*This* must be the hidden treasure – everything he stole over the years!"

The curator took her glasses from the top of her head and perched them on her nose as she flipped through the diary. I noticed several of the special guests among the crowd beginning to slip away, including Redbeard, and wondered what they all had to hide. Ms Boyd's pencilled eyebrows crept higher and higher and her bright red lips formed a shocked little "O" as she kept reading.

"Goodness. The list goes on and on. A tiara from Dame Wessington when she had an ancient woodland felled on her land because she thought a nest of rare owls were glaring at her. Three gold rings from Sir Hawxley because he objected to the new children's hospital being built because he thought children were a waste of space. Oh dear, there are names and deeds I hardly dare mention."

The press closed in.

"Mention them!"

"Give us more names!"

"What did they do?"

"What else did he steal?"

"Where did he hide the loot?"

"Say no more!" shouted a man as the

crowd surged forward. "*The Bugle* will pay for exclusive rights to serialise the diary!"

Ms Boyd held up her hands. "My loves, much as we all long to know, there's nothing here that tells us where to find his hoard. So for now, I'm afraid the show is over."

SHOW'S OVER! ON WITH THE SHOW! cried Cookie, then whistled the circus clown theme Dad had taught him. I tried shushing him, but everyone was laughing and Cookie loved attention.

"So, what did happen to Harrington's money?" called the journalist from *The Bugle*.

"Hah! It was never missing." Orion laughed. "He left it to a wonderful scheme for rehabilitating young offenders. And now I see why! It was to make up for his own crimes!"

"Unbelievable!" burst out the reporter as the crowd rocked with laughter.

"Unbelievable – that was Harry." Orion smiled.

"Now, we must bid you farewell as we close the gallery and this incredible exhibition," announced Ms Boyd as the laughter finally died down. "Thank you, darlings, for attending this most extraordinary evening. Congratulations again to Rani and her nani!"

The crowd cheered until Ms Boyd finally gave Charity a nod and the security guard chivvied the remaining journalists and guests towards the exits.

I caught up with Lexi and Ollie as they were leaving. "Thanks for telling people that we hadn't come back from Signal Rock. Without you, Mrs Rutter would probably have used Cookie to get the clue items out of us and then left us trapped out there."

Lexi smiled and raised an eyebrow. "Maybe you could reward us with an exclusive Steel Reveals interview?"

I smiled and shook her hand. "It's a deal."

"Goodness, my dears, what an afternoon!" Ms Boyd mopped her brow with a little handkerchief.

"Well, well," said Orion. "This explains why he never fired Mrs Rutter. I'll bet it amused old Harry that someone was stealing from *him* too. I can't believe he managed to keep his delinquency

250

from me." He clapped me on the back and reached out to shake hands with Nani. "Well done, both of you. That was some entrance."

Nani swept him up into one of her big, squeezy bear hugs. "Thank you for stopping that terrible woman from taking the prize and disappearing."

"That's quite all right," said Orion struggling to get away, then giving in to Nani's unbreakable hug. "Though in the end, a lighthouse isn't exactly something she could just disappear into the sunset with!"

"It's a shame we may never know where Lord Harrington hid his loot," said Ms Boyd. "There must be millions of pounds' worth of stolen treasures hidden away."

I had been thinking about this last puzzle. Why was it so important that the diary was brought here before the exhibition ended? Something was itching at my brain.

I left Orion and Ms Boyd talking and wandered over to the brightly coloured heads in Lord Harrington's exhibition. I was still puzzled about why he had bothered to cast plaster heads rather than painting the carved wooden versions they were moulded from. Unless… Things began to fall into place.

"What's up, Coco?" said Nani, sidling over to me as I stared up at the big, square chin on the bust of a man with a huge moustache.

"These faces. I'm sure this one is meant to be the mayor and that one, in the big earrings…"

"Looks just like Lady Hardright," finished Nani. She peered closely at the busts. "Then the one with the tiara must be Dame Wessington."

"And this one here, with his chin on his fist," I said, gesturing to the bust of a man who looked as though he was sucking pickled lemons. "There are three rings on his fingers – it has to be Sir Hawxley."

I grinned at Nani. "Are you thinking what I'm thinking?"

"It would be just the kind of thing I'd expect from that old trickster!" Nani laughed.

I reached up to lift Lady Hardright's head from its plinth.

"What are you doing?" shouted Ms Boyd, hurrying over. "Don't touch those. They're works of art!"

"But they're not," I said as the curator whisked me away from the statues.

"You may not appreciate them, but those are some of Lord Harrington's last artworks. They must be preserved."

"But I think I know where…"

"Rani, my dear, sweet chicken, this has been an exciting day for us all, but now it's time to go home and rest our weary heads. Mrs Ballah… it was a delight to meet you. Now if you would please follow me…"

Nani wasn't listening. A look of complete innocence spread over her face. She winked at me, then tottered over as though falling in slow motion. I pulled out my camera, switched it to video mode and began recording as Nani teetered straight into a plinth and knocked Lady Hardright's head to the floor with a deafening crash.

Ms Boyd let out a horrified little yelp and Cookie flew off to a safe perch on one of the picture rails as a cloud of white dust poofed up from the broken bust.

Ms Boyd's ringed fingers gripped my shoulders tightly as Nani spun across the room in a ridiculous pretend fall, knocking over plinths and statues like dominoes, caught up in the joy of *finally* getting to smash something. Soon she was almost hidden by a giant cloud of white dust as everything crumbled into rubble around her.

WHOOPS-A-DAISY, cackled Cookie. CALL THE COPS!

"What have you done?!" wailed Ms Boyd, hands clasped to her chest. Orion and Charles hurried over and helped Nani to her feet.

"Mersi." Nani shook the powder from her tunic. "No bones broken."

"Your bones are the only things unbroken!" cried Ms Boyd. "You've destroyed Lord Harrington's sculpture collection!"

"Don't worry," said Nani. "They can be cast again using the moulds we found at the lighthouse."

"Besides," I said as I handed Nani my camera. "These were meant to be broken. I'll show you why." I dropped to my knees and scrabbled through the rubble, sifting the powder through my fingers. Just as I began to worry that I might have been wrong and we had destroyed the artworks for nothing, Cookie swept down to snatch up something glimmering red and gold in the dust.

"Clever Cookie," I called. "Bring it to Rani."

He flapped down to my wrist and, with only a tiny struggle, I took the item from his beak, wiped it on my jumper and handed it to Ms Boyd.

"Bet you a bazillion pounds that's one of Lady Hardright's ruby earrings," I said.

"And here's the other!" cried Orion, crumbling the remainder of a plaster ear in his hand to reveal another earring.

"I don't believe it!" Ms Boyd turned the earring over in her hand as I dived back into the rubble with Nani, Charles and Orion. Together we crumbled chunks of plaster to uncover treasure after treasure. Rings, diamond bracelets and necklaces, a gold cigar cutter, even a tube containing a carefully rolled Picasso sketch.

Finally, Ms Boyd couldn't hold herself back and leaped in to join the fun. Her stylish ballerina skirt was soon completely white. She squealed with joy when she smashed open Dame Wessington's head to reveal her tiara.

Before long, all of the busts had been smashed to dust and a pile of treasure sparkled on the floor.

Ms Boyd laughed as we brushed plaster from our clothes, looking very much like statues ourselves. "Darling girl, how did you know that was where the treasure was hidden?"

"I guessed hiding the stolen loot in plain sight would be just the kind of final trick Lord Harrington would enjoy playing on everyone."

"You can say that again," said a voice. I spun round to see Camera Guy watching us with a grin.

"Will!" Orion jumped up to shake his hand. "Rani, Sita, this is Will Baxter. He's a journalist and filmmaker. Old Harry wanted him to document the search for the diary. I imagine he'll be keen to take you back to the lighthouse for photos."

"Once you've recovered from your adventuring!" Will smiled. He shook our powdery hands and then we all posed in the rubble with handfuls of treasure as he snapped a few pictures.

"I'm sure Lord Harrington loved the idea of his sculptures being destroyed to reveal his hoard," said Will as he checked through his pictures.

"And I've recorded the moment it happened as his final piece of art," I added. "With Nani as the star!"

"Wonderful!" Ms Boyd cried. "It will be his finest work yet!"

"I've never met such a trickster in my entire life," said Orion. "And I doubt I ever will again. Oh, I do miss old Harry."

CHAPTER SIXTEEN

Rani Reports

"We're famous, Coco," said Nani as she pinned yet another news clipping to the noticeboard in our kitchen. The landline had hardly stopped ringing since the events at the gallery. National newspapers called to interview me, and we went back to the lighthouse with Will and a camera crew, who filmed us talking about Lord Harrington's puzzle trail.

I did my exclusive interview with Lexi, although I'd kept back some important parts of the story for my own article for the Junior Journalist competition. In any case, Lexi wanted her reveal to focus on me and Nani, the attempted burglary, Cookie's birdnapping and how we cracked the clues, obviously with a bit of exaggeration of her and Ollie's role in our rescue from Signal Rock.

But I felt that the real story wasn't about me. It was in what the treasure hunt revealed about Lord Harrington's life and him as a person – Olympian, philanthropist, vigilante thief and everything in between.

The piece took me two whole days to write, especially as people kept calling for interviews. It was very hard to fit everything that had happened into five hundred words, but I had hit the word count exactly and submitted my entry minutes before the deadline on Sunday night. I'd taken a few tips from Lexi and used exciting language and hooks to keep the reader interested, but had made sure to quote everyone exactly and check all of my facts. I got quotes from Orion, Billy and even Nani to give a range of perspectives on Lord Harrington.

Billy had really had no idea what Mrs Rutter was up to and was very upset that she'd pretended he was involved in her plot. He had sent over a bunch of flowers from Harrington Hall's gardens. The groundskeeper wasn't nearly as grumpy as he looked. I was glad to hear he'd be keeping his job at Harrington Hall and looked forward to visiting his gardens again, though not as much as I was looking forward to visiting the lighthouse.

It was Monday afternoon. Nani and I were sitting at the kitchen table eating mine frire – fried noodles – and staring up at the latest newspaper article we had pinned to the corkboard:

UNIVERSITY RECEIVES STELLAR SURPRISE

I'd loved seeing the galaxy from the lighthouse's observatory and felt I couldn't keep the universe to myself. So, with Nani's help, my first act as the guardian of Signal Rock was to offer the local university permission to use the observatory for their cosmology and astrology research. I'd also offered to let them borrow the *Dancing Deacon* to take students there, along with members of the public, for free astronomy lectures. I'd still have lots of opportunities to visit the lighthouse myself during school holidays and could call on experts whenever I needed help exploring the skies.

A car horn beeped outside.

BEEP-BEEEEP. CALL THE COPS! squawked Cookie from the fruit bowl as she nibbled the lychees Nani had just put in there.

The door flew open and Mum and Dad swept into the kitchen.

"We're baaa-aaack!" shouted Dad.

"And the house is still standing!" said Mum.

"Welcome home!" said Nani, placing a bowl of freshly fried gato pima chilli cakes on the table.

"Hi, Mum! Hi, Dad." I squeaked as they lifted me up and planted kisses all over my face.

KiSSY-KiSSY, MWAH, MWAH! squawked Cookie, bouncing up and down on the kitchen counter.

"Kisses for you too," said Dad, giving him a peck on the beak.

"It's so nice to be home," Mum kicked off her shoes, sunk into the armchair and patted the arm for me to sit next to her. "I hope you've been helping Nani while we've been away."

"Actually, I've been helping Rani," said Nani, beaming. She held up today's copy of the *Camberford Herald*. "A little surprise for you, Coco." My hands flew to my cheeks as I saw what was printed on the front cover:

THE TRICKSTER'S TREASURE

by Rani Ramgoolam

"My article! But how?" I asked Nani. "Did I win?"

"They haven't judged the competition yet," said Nani. "But they loved your article and wanted to print it while the story was still fresh. They called this morning and I told them that they could. I hope you don't mind me keeping it from you. I wanted it to be a surprise."

"It's the best surprise ever!" I wrapped my arms around her waist as she handed the paper to Mum and Dad. I was a journalist. A real journalist, with my first article on the front page of the paper. What better start could I have?

"What is this?" asked Mum. She looked at Dad and read out a quote I'd taken from Nani for the article.

"That trickster sent us on quite the journey to discover his secret and loot," Mrs Ballah said. "From a study full of secrets, to a minotaur's maze, a lonely lighthouse and a high-tech bank vault. All that time, the treasure was sitting right back where we started, and we had a smashing time uncovering it!"

Mum and Dad finished reading my article.

"You… You wrote this?" said Mum, holding up the paper.

"And solved these riddles all by yourselves?" Dad waved his hand at all the clippings about our discovery pinned to the kitchen corkboard.

"And you won a *lighthouse*?" Mum shook her head. "A real lighthouse?"

"Sort of!" I grinned. "I'm its guardian until I'm old and grey like you two."

"The cheek!" I dodged as Dad reached out to tickle me, then I pulled the *Dancing Deacon*'s keys from my pocket. "Would you like to see it? Nani can take us in our new motorboat."

"Ayo!" Mum clapped her hands to her face. The paper slid from her lap. "My mother, behind the wheel of a boat!"

"Don't worry," said Nani. "We'll take extra fuel so we don't get stranded at sea again."

"AGAIN?" cried Mum and Dad together as I made a *shushy* face at Nani from behind them.

AYO! screeched Cookie as Mum jumped to her feet.

"That's **IT**, Ma!" she exploded. "That's the last time we leave you two alone. No more adventures, investigations, or story-chasing for either of you!"

Nani caught my eye as Mum went on with her list of forbidden activities. She winked and we shared a secret smile. With so many exciting stories out there just waiting to be chased, we wouldn't be making any promises.

THE TRICKSTER'S TREASURE

by Rani Ramgoolam

Lord Rupert Harrington was many things: Olympic gymnast, Formula One cup winner, mountain climber, author, philanthropist, artist, sailor. But a diary, containing a dire secret, revealed one role he hid from the world...vigilante thief.

On passing away in January at ninety years old, Lord Harrington left a generous donation to the Bayley Art Gallery on condition that an exhibition of his artwork was held there as soon as it could be scheduled after his demise. The centrepiece of this exhibition? A self-portrait containing the first clue in a trail which would lead to a diary hidden deep in the vaults of Grennards bank.

Within this diary, Lord Harrington confessed to millions of pounds' worth of thefts from prominent figures such as Dame Wessington, Sir Hawxley and Mayor Slater. Adding insult to injury, the loot was hidden within grotesque caricatures of their owners. What drove Camberford's richest bachelor to become a thief?

"He would get quite philosophical during our chats in the gardens," said Billy McTavish, groundskeeper of the Harrington estate. "Ten years ago, he told me, 'The rich can get away with almost anything, Billy. Too many take advantage of that. I'd like to teach some people how it feels to be on the receiving end for once.' I laughed, but it seems he wasn't joking."

That moment marked the beginning of Lord Harrington's decade of crime–stealing from those he believed were getting away with deplorable actions. While some believe this behaviour was out of character, those closest to the peer weren't completely shocked.

"Old Harry had a strong sense of justice and couldn't bear rudeness or bigotry," said Orion Aldridge, manager of Grennards bank and friend of Lord Harrington. "I would never have suspected him of being a vigilante thief, but knowing his thrill-seeking, mischievous nature, and belief in fair play, I can't say I'm totally surprised."

The hoard of stolen treasures was discovered by ten-year-old Rani Ramgoolam and her grandmother Sita Ballah, currently visiting Camberford from Fond du Sac, Mauritius.

"That trickster sent us on quite the journey to discover his secret,"

Mrs Ballah said. "From a study full of secrets, to a minotaur's maze, a lonely lighthouse and a high-tech bank vault. All that time, the loot was sitting right back where we started, and we had a smashing time uncovering it!"

Camberford police have announced that the stolen property has been returned to its rightful owners, all of whom declined to offer a quote for this article. However, since Lord Harrington's diary was made public, many of his victims have made large, public donations to charitable causes. Sir Hawxley to the children's hospital, Mayor Slater to the Cat's Protection League and Dame Wessington to the Forestry Commission.

Even Lord Harrington himself tried to atone for his crimes by donating his entire fortune to a scheme for helping young offenders find work and learn new skills.

Lord Harrington's final revelation and explosive exhibition has left Camberford reeling. Whether people are shocked, delighted, furious or confused, everyone is talking about his tricks. From what this reporter has learned over the last week, that's all old Harry would have wanted.

READ ALL ABOUT IT!

Now that you've read Rani's article, why not have a go at writing a story of your own? You could write up an article based on Rani and Nani's adventure, or on a real-life event that you think is important or newsworthy.

News articles all have a similar format. They start with a catchy **headline** in bold. Consider alliteration for something that rolls off the tongue.

MONKEY MAYHEM IN MIDDLESBROUGH!

This is the headline and it is followed by the **byline,** which is the line that tells us who the article is by.

by Jessica Journalist

After this comes the **lead**. This is a paragraph that contains the most important information and sums up the story.

> Yesterday, Teesside residents were shocked when a troop of monkeys escaped from Edinburgh Zoo, stole a tour bus, and stopped in Middlesbrough on their way down to London. Shopkeepers barricaded their doors as the monkeys raided all of the town's fruit and veg shops. The monkeys finally got back on the road after a two-hour feeding frenzy in which they ate every banana in Middlesbrough.

In the **body** of the article you cover the important details of the story. What happened? How does it affect people? You could also write quotes from witnesses or people involved. Be sure to get your facts straight and don't jump to conclusions like Lexi Steel!

The **tail** of the story contains any extra information, often the background to the story, any events leading up to it. In this case, it might look at how the monkeys escaped from the zoo.

Your article should be written in the past tense and end with a couple of lines that sum up the story. It could possibly finish with the journalist's opinion (yours!).

NANI'S GATO PIMA CHILLI CAKES RECIPE

Gato Pima, which translates as "chilli cakes", are a very popular snack in Mauritius. They've very easy and cheap to make, and a bit like falafel but made with yellow split peas instead of chickpeas.

INGREDIENTS

250g yellow split peas
Soaked overnight then rinsed and drained

2 tablespoons fresh coriander
Chopped

2–3 spring onions
Finely chopped bulbs and leaves

1 green and 1 red chilli
Finely chopped – remove seeds to make it less spicy, add more chillies if you like heat!

1 teaspoon cumin powder

½ teaspoon salt

Oil for frying
You'll need an adult to do this bit!

PREPARING THE YELLOW SPLIT PEAS

Pop the drained split peas in a food processor in a few batches and grind to a paste. It's important that you don't make it all too smooth. Finely ground peas help the mix stick together, chunkier bits give it a lovely texture and crunch!

MAKING THE CHILLI CAKES

Put the ground peas into a bowl, add the spring onions, chillies, coriander, spring onions and salt, then give it all a really good mix together.

Using a desert spoon, scoop out some of the mix and shape it into a little ball. Squeeze between thumb and forefinger to flatten slightly, leaving an indentation on either side. This helps the chilli cakes to cook all the way through so that they're nice and crunchy! Do the same with the rest of the mix. You should end up with around 20–25.

Get an adult to heat enough oil in a pan or wok to float the chilli cakes, then fry them in batches until golden brown. Adjust the heat as needed.

Scoop the cooked gato pima out on to a plate lined with kitchen roll to drain the excess oil.

Allow to cool for a while, then gobble them up while they're still warm!

TIPS

In Mauritius, gato pima are often dipped in a chutney made from half a bunch of coriander, a tomato, a green chilli and a bit of salt, all pureed together. You can leave the chilli out if the cakes are already spicy enough for you.

Leftover gato pima can be cooked up in a curry sauce, like veggie meatballs, in a dish called cari bari, or broken up into the chutney and eaten in a baguette.

GLOSSARY

Most Mauritians speak two or three languages. Mauritian Creole is a French-based language which most people use at home. French is more commonly used at work and school. English is also used in school, Parliament and by people in the tourism industry. You will also hear a mix of Indian and Chinese languages spoken, among many others! Here are the words used by Rani and her family in this book.

Ki manyer?	How are you?	Key man-yeah
Ayo!	Exclamation of surprise or dismay	Eye-oh
Coco	A term of endearment	
Zoli	Beautiful	Zoh-lee
Manzer	Eat	Mon-zay
Chalo!	Let's go!	Cha-low. *Hindi*
Mersi	Thanks	Mer-see
Mamou	Uncle	Mam-oo. *Hindi*

FOOD

Mine Frire	Fried noodles	Min free-er
Gato pima	Chilli cakes	Ga-toe pea-ma
Gato patate	Potato cakes	Ga-toe pat-at
Roti	Round flatbread	Roh-tea
Rougail	Spicy tomato sauce	Roe-guy

THANKS!

We hope you enjoyed reading Rani and Nani's first adventure as much as we enjoyed writing it! Now it's time to say a few words to some special people.

GABRIELLE: The very first draft of this book was finished while I was living in James Cook Hospital for a month before our daughter was born. Satish visited every day and we would chat about the story and the adventures we would soon have with our own daughter. I'd like to thank him for working with me on this series and sharing his brilliant ideas and for his amazing planning, editorial and problem-solving skills. Thanks also to all of the staff at the hospital who helped keep our daughter safe on her way into this world. While writing away, I shared a room with Chelsea Wilkinson, the bravest mum I have ever met. I told her I'd mention her equally brave boys, William and Joe, in this book, and hope Josie Anne and Joshua Dean enjoy the story I finished writing in the bed across from their mum.

SATISH: I'd like to thank my father, Somduth, for teaching me to read and for pushing me to write creatively ever since my very first composition, "Hedgey the Hedgehog". And my mother, Anusuya, for being a real-world Nani, taking us all on adventures and ensuring we never went too long without gato pima. A huge thanks to Gabrielle for getting all of our ideas down in words and encouraging me to share my experience as a first generation British-Mauritian.

We are both very grateful to our superstar agent, Hannah Sheppard, for sending Rani out into the world and to our publisher, Rock the Boat, particularly our editor Katie Jennings for her great ideas and advice, which really helped us to elevate this story, and the rest of Team Rani Reports: Lucy, Mark, Paul, Laura, Deontaye, Beth and Ben.

We were very pleased that *Rani Reports* is the debut book for our ace illustrator, Navya Raju. Navya has done a brilliant job of visualising Rani's world, and in many cases her interpretation of characters are better than the visions we had in our heads! We're very much looking forward to seeing what she comes up with for the rest of the series.

Sending lots of gratitude to our family at home and around the world for their support, cheerleading and for providing real life inspiration for our characters. Also to all of the brilliant authors who have supported us, and the awesome librarians, teachers and booksellers who share our stories with readers like you. And to a few special teachers who shared wonderful stories with us and directly inspired us to write – Vin Early, Brenda Harrison, Mr Hughes and many more.

Finally, a big thank you to YOU for joining Rani and Nani on this adventure. We hope you'll follow them as they get into lots more trouble together!

Keep your eyes peeled
for Rani and Nani's next investigation in

RANI REPORTS
ON THE COPYCAT CRIMES

COMING YOUR WAY
JUNE 2024

GABRIELLE & SATISH SHEWHORAK

Satish was born in the Wirral to parents from the tropical island of Mauritius. Gabrielle was born in County Durham to an Irish mum and English dad and has family all over the globe. As children's authors, they would love every child to be able to recognise themselves in the characters they see in books, games and film.

Before becoming a full-time writer, Gabrielle was a videogame developer and lecturer. Satish ran an animation studio before earning a PhD in motion capture and now teaches videogame animation. They first met in Tokyo where they tested each other's gaming skills in late night videogame arcades. They live in the North of England and have a wonderful young daughter who has just started hogging their games consoles – they couldn't be prouder! Gabrielle also writes middle grade under the name Gabrielle Kent, including Knights and Bikes, and the Alfie Bloom series.

NAVYA RAJU

Navya Raju is an illustrator-storyteller based in Hyderabad, a multicultural city in India, with an academic background in architecture. Her works are influenced by architecture, cinema, literature, and pretty much everything and anything that fascinates her. When she's not drawing or writing you can find her making some really fun playlists, collecting quirky trinkets and stationery, and hopping around new bakeries in town.